SILK QUEEN

BOOK I & II

G. J. WALKER-SMITH

PART I

CHAPTER 1

I WAS PRACTICALLY RAISED IN MY MOTHER'S HABERDASHERY shop. As a result, I know far too much about needles, thread and buttons, but not much about anything else.

Nellie's Needle is a tiny shop that is overstocked and disorganised, but the location is decent, on a main road crammed between a tobacconist and a baker. It wasn't exactly Harrods, but what would I know? I'd never been to Harrods. I'd never left Manchester. Life in my hometown of Denton wasn't exactly charmed. I helped out in my mother's shop and did a bit of house cleaning in nearby Stockport in a bid to earn extra money.

Weddings are expensive and I wanted mine to be perfect, just like Princess Di's. In fairness, mine probably wasn't going to be anywhere near as grand as hers. A beautiful gown with a twenty-five-foot train was out of the question – no amount of saving would stretch the budget that far.

My vision of flowy silk gave way to stiff taffeta, and my resourceful mother fashioned a floor length veil out of a pair of lace curtains off the shop floor. The end result was a simple white dress with fake pearl buttons and a puffy skirt.

"Wait until Andrew sees it," exclaimed my mother. "He'll fall in love with you all over again."

I couldn't actually remember Andrew falling in love with me the first time around. Sparks didn't fly when our eyes met across a crowded dance floor – there was no meeting. I'd known him my whole life, and now we were getting married. To me, it sounded more like the end of the story rather than the beginning but my mother wouldn't hear of it.

"You need to stop reading those romance novels, my girl," she scolded. "They're ruining your mind."

Romance novels didn't ruin me. They were my escape, and the biggest lesson I was ever likely to get on how it felt to fall fiercely and blindly in love.

DIARY OF FIONA BLACK

FRIDAY JULY 15, 1983

Today I sold Mrs Wimbush a set of curtains that were exactly the same as my veil. Surely Princess Di's veil cost more than £8?
I'm going out with the girls tomorrow. Charlene's going to pick up a couple of bottles at the off-license after work. Gill's closer, but she's been banned from going in there until she apologises.
Andrew's going to Stretford with a mate but wouldn't say who or why. I bet it's Trevor. He knows I hate that knob.
Book of the week: My Darling Lover
Honeymoon fund: £64.

CHAPTER 2

MY FRIEND CHARLENE IS THE POSHEST GIRL I'VE EVER KNOWN. Her father is a bank manager and her mother has a genuine Liz Claiborne handbag. We first met when my mam enrolled me in Brownies when I was six. Once a week we'd meet up at the school hall and do our best to pretend that we were upstanding and conscientious girls. The Brownie phase was over by the time I turned ten, but my friendship with Charlene endured.

I wish I was more like her, and almost always tried to be. It wasn't just her fancy clothes or stylish perm that made her classy. Her accent was dead posh too, and that was the thing I tried hardest to emulate. I was never going to live at Buckingham Palace, but I could at least pretend that I did.

My friend Gill didn't give a hoot about sounding posh. Accents didn't matter in reform school, and Gill would know. She'd been sent down twice before – once for joyriding in a stolen car and again for shoplifting a few months later.

To her credit, she's stayed out of trouble for a while now. Once we turned eighteen, the threat of a stint in Borstal no

7

longer applied. Riding in stolen cars with boys would now earn her a stint in proper jail, and not even Gill was that tough.

She pulled her head in and signed up for a secretarial course at the local college, and after failing twice, she was finally gearing up to graduate. That was the reason for tonight's celebration. The three of us met up at one of our usual haunts – the playground at the nursery school on Grove Road.

Gill was there when I arrived, dragging her Doc Martins through the dirt as she slowly spun on the roundabout.

"Hiya. You alright?"

She lifted her head and smiled. "Better than alright." She waved something at me. "I just found 50p in the sand. Rich little bastards at this school."

I giggled my way over to the swing. "Keep digging. I have a honeymoon to pay for."

Gill grimaced at the reminder. "A waste of time and money," she muttered.

To her, getting married at twenty was the most ridiculous idea on earth. No matter how many times I defended the decision, I never managed to convince her otherwise. There wasn't time to try today. Charlene appeared, tottering across the yard in her white stilettos carrying a big green bottle.

"About bloody time," said Gill, jumping to her feet. "A girl could die of thirst."

"You each owe me 30p," replied Charlene, handing it to her.

Green Totty Cider was hardly top shelf, but we were skint and it was cheap.

The bottle hissed as Gill twisted the lid. "Last of the big spenders, aren't we?"

Spending Saturday nights drinking in the playground in summer was nothing out of the ordinary for us. As far as behaviour went, it was as top shelf as our drink of choice, but old habits are hard to break.

"Do you think we'll still come here when I'm married?" I asked. "It's probably not the done thing, right?"

I directed the question at Charlene, but Gill jumped in. "As if Andrew will care," she scoffed. "Where is he tonight anyway?"

"Stretford," I replied. "With Trevor."

She handed me the bottle. "Ugh! Bloody Trevor."

"Have you seen him lately?" asked Charlene. "He has a moustache now. It looks like a giant bat flew up his nose."

"It's his Magnum P.I. look," said Gill, cackling.

Trevor Hillman – and blokes like him – were the main reason we stayed out of the pubs on a Saturday night. He was a creep. He also happened to be my fiancé's best mate.

"He's going to be best man at my wedding." I pulled a face, slightly horrified by the prospect.

Charlene sat down next to Gill on the roundabout, seemingly oblivious that her pristine white stilettos were digging into the sand. "Make sure he gets rid of the 'tache."

Gill leaned, taking the bottle from my grasp. "Just call it all off." She threw her head back and took a giant gulp before speaking again. "Getting married is stupid."

More than once, I'd wondered if her negativity stemmed from jealousy. I had a lot to be envious of, and for the first time ever, I called her out on it.

"You think I'm jealous?" she asked, eyes wide. "I think you're a knob for even considering it. You're throwing your whole life away."

"I love him, Gill."

"Love is overrated," she shot back.

"Maybe you've just never been in love," suggested Charlene.

Gill handed her the bottle of cider. "Tell me what it's like then," she demanded. "What's the big fuss about?"

Charlene looked across at me, rapidly blinking as if she had sand in her eye. "I don't know what it's like," she admitted. "I've never been in love either."

I wasn't good with words, but I liked them. I grabbed my bag and reached for the tatty Mills and Boon novel that I kept hidden in the side pocket.

I thumbed through to the chapter I was looking for and geared up to enlighten them both. "At that moment, Perdita knew that Mario was the only man she'd want for the rest of her life," I read out loud. "As she looked into his chestnut brown eyes, her heart began thumping. Her body trembled, overcome with pure wanton desire."

"What the flippin' 'eck is wanton desire?" interrupted Gill. "And Perdita is a naff name."

Charlene bumped her with her shoulder. "Shut up and let her read."

I cleared my throat and continued. "Mario leaned closer, touching his warm lips to Perdita's ear. 'I must go,' he breathed. 'But when you hear the cold wind howling in the distance, know that it is I, whispering your name.'"

Gill groaned as if her belly hurt. Charlene stretched the bottom of her grey knitted dress to cover her knees. "That was lovely, Fi," she praised, almost sincerely. "Is that how you feel about Andrew?"

I felt my shoulders sag as I silently answered her question. The only thing that ever made my body tremble was cheap Green Totty Cider. But I was a realist. My mother had told me a hundred times that life is not a fairy-tale.

I wasn't Princess Di. There was no Prince Charles on my horizon. My prince was an apprentice bricklayer from Denton.

Andrew was no wind-whispering Mario, but he was real and he was good and he loved me. That had to be enough.

DIARY OF FIONA BLACK

SATURDAY JULY 16, 1983

Never drinking again. Cider is poison. Threw up in the pot plant near the door on the way in.

Charl is in worse shape. Gill asked her if she felt ok and Charl told her to sod off. Charlene never says sod off.

<u>Book of the week:</u> My Darling Lover

<u>Honeymoon fund:</u> £63.20

CHAPTER 3

I FIRST MET MRS CRICHTON-PERCY WHEN SHE VISITED MY mother's shop. Mam told her that I was getting married (because Mam tells everybody), then mentioned that I was on the scrounge for extra work.

In a stroke of pure luck, Mrs Crichton-Percy was looking for a part time house cleaner.

It was the perfect arrangement. Three afternoons a week, I caught the 372 bus out to Bramhall and spent a few hours cleaning an already spotless house.

The rest of the time was usually spent daydreaming that I lived there. The big Tudor home was magnificent. Each of the five bedrooms had its own private bathroom, and there was a games room with a pool table just like the one in the Gloucester Arms Pub.

Mrs Crichton-Percy was a kind lady, which was a good thing because I took a few liberties. I often sneaked a squirt of the Chloé perfume on her dresser and was constantly checking out her shoe collection. When she walked in on me in her bedroom that day, I was parading in front of the mirror wearing a pink pillbox hat that I'd found at the top of her wardrobe.

"I wore that to the races at Aintree last year," she told me.

"I'm sorry," I stammered, snatching it off my head. "I couldn't resist trying it on."

Mrs Crichton-Percy slid open the mirrored wardrobe door and began raking hangers across the rail. "I wore it with this." She turned, holding a dead lovely drop-waisted pink dress.

"It's beautiful." I practically moaned out the compliment. "I really like the sequined bow."

She smiled at me. "We all deserve a bit of glamour in our lives, don't you think?"

I was nodding before she even got the question out.

There was a rueful tinge to Mrs Crichton-Percy's smile. Perhaps she knew that gawking at her race day outfit was as close to glitz as I was likely to get.

"I have something you might like," she suggested, walking over to the big chest of drawers near the window.

I stood firm, holding my breath in anticipation, and when she turned around and presented me with a small sequined clutch bag I nearly squealed. "It's gorgeous!"

"Your first piece of designer glitz," she announced. "The first of many, I'm sure."

I thanked her a hundred times, painfully aware of how stupid I sounded.

"And something to put in it," she added, handing me five quid.

My weekly housecleaning wage felt a like highway robbery at times. I worked far harder in Mam's shop for much less reward, but I was always grateful to receive it. It brought us one step closer to our dream honeymoon. And if we ever did make the bright lights of Blackpool, I'd have a dead posh handbag to take with me.

I stood at the end of the Crichton-Percys' driveway and waited for Andrew to pick me up, grasping my new little bag with both hands. I squared my shoulders and held my head high as if I was the lady of the manor waiting on her driver. As expected, the daydream quickly slipped.

I heard Andrew's car before I saw it. There was no mistaking the sound of a souped-up Ford Cortina with a dodgy exhaust. It was downright embarrassing, especially in this neighbourhood.

He leaned over and threw open the passenger door. "Hiya, lass."

After clearing a pile of junk off the seat, I got in the car. "I thought you were going to get that noise fixed."

"I am."

"When?"

He took my hand and kissed it. "One day."

Everything was going to happen one day. My mam called Andrew grounded. "That lad's good for you," she constantly assured me. "He keeps your head out of the clouds."

I looked down at the sequined bag in my lap, glinting in the afternoon sun. "See what I got today?" I asked. "It's a Mel Lazar bag. She's a famous designer."

Andrew reached over and swept his hand through my hair. "You're turning into a right posh lass," he teased. "I can't keep up with you."

His eyes never left the road as I gazed at him. Twenty-one-year-old Andrew was boyishly handsome with a devilish smile.

I loved him, but he was right. I didn't think he could keep up with me either, and it sometimes scared me.

DIARY OF FIONA BLACK

MONDAY JULY 18, 1983

*I wonder how posh people like Mrs Crichton-Percy end up with
double-barrelled surnames. Maybe they make it up themselves.
I could never do that.*

*Andrew's last name is bad enough. I certainly don't want to make it
worse by being Fiona Black-Pidgeon.*

*Mam found the puke in the pot plant. I blamed the cat from next
door. She said someone needs to find the cat and put it out of its
misery.*

Book of the week: My Darling Lover
Honeymoon fund: £68.20

CHAPTER 4

THERE'S A REASON WHY PEOPLE LIKE MRS CRICHTON-PERCY shopped for fabric at Nellie's Needle. My mother stocked some of the finest dress fabrics this side of London. How she managed to get hold of them was anyone's guess, but mine was that they fell off the back of a truck.

Her latest acquisition was two bolts of beautiful black dupioni silk. I noticed them instantly, sticking out like a sore thumb against the cheap voile and taffeta.

I picked up a roll and held it close as I waltzed down the narrow aisle. "All of my dresses will be made of silk like this one day," I wistfully declared.

"At ten quid a yard?" scoffed my mother. "You're marrying the wrong Andrew. Head to the palace and set your sights on the prince instead."

I leaned the roll of fabric against the wall. "I don't fancy Prince Andrew, Mam," I muttered. "He's not the marrying kind."

My mother chuckled her way to the front of the store, flipped over the sign on the door and declared Nellie's Needle open for the day.

~

THE PROMISE I MADE OF WORKING THE ENTIRE DAY ONLY HELD until eleven. Andrew appeared at the front window, calling me outside with a wave of his hand and a cheeky smile.

I quickly glanced across at my mother, who was at the counter explaining her no-refund policy to Mrs Boorman.

"There's nowt wrong with them, Missus," she gruffly insisted.

"They hang crooked," came the fast reply.

My mother pushed the folded curtains back across the counter. "You go home and tell your Fred to put the rail up straight," she ordered. "He hung it on a lean."

It was entirely possible. Mr Boorman only had one eye.

As riveting as the conversation was, I wanted to get out of there. Asking permission to leave was pointless, so I didn't. While Mam was occupied, I slipped out the door.

Nellie Black was not to be underestimated. If she'd wanted to chase me down and drag me back by the hair, she would've. Andrew knew it too, which is why he grabbed my hand and took off running down the road.

"Run, Fi!" he ordered. I could barely breathe for laughing. "If she catches us, there's no telling what she'll do."

If Mam did give chase, she wasn't quick enough. The beaten up white Cortina with the red stripe along the side was parked around the corner, idling at the ready. We jumped in and Andrew floored it, and in a plume of choking white smoke, we took off down the road.

"Where to, lass?" he asked.

I ducked my head, looking up through the cracked windscreen at the bright sky above. It was a glorious day, and I could think of no better way to spend it than in the sunshine with my fiancé.

The park is where we ended up – not too far from home, but far enough away to feel like we'd truly escaped. We ran through the gates as if there was still a chance that Mam was chasing us, bolting across the lawn until our breath ran out. I finally tumbled onto the grass in a heap and Andrew flopped down beside me.

Keeping my focus on the sky above, I reached for his hand. "Why aren't you at work today?" I asked.

I didn't need to look at him to know he was smiling. I could hear it in his voice. "I'm dead poorly," he claimed. "Too hungover to cart bricks."

Andrew wasn't the most conscientious apprentice that ever lived. In fact, he skived work more often than he turned up. The reason why he was never sacked was simple – he worked for his uncle Ed, who was just as slack as him.

"We're supposed to be saving for Blackpool," I grumbled. "Lazy git."

There's a fine line between procrastinating and being bone-idle. I was wound far too tightly to tolerate either – and it didn't seem to bother Andrew in the slightest.

"I have something for you." He reached into his jeans pocket, pulled out a crisp ten-pound note and tucked it down the front of my top. "Put it away for a rainy Blackpool day."

As far as romantic gestures go, it was as grand as Andrew's get. I was thrilled – so thrilled that I threw myself on top of him.

His arms slipped around me. "I'll always do the best I can for you, Fi," he quietly promised.

I dropped my head and softly kissed him. "I know," I murmured.

Over time, I'd come to realise that no matter how hard I wished for it, life wasn't going to imitate the pages of my romance novels.

Andrew wasn't perfect, but he made me happy and that was enough. When the need for perfection hit me, I'd always have my books.

DIARY OF FIONA BLACK

TUESDAY JULY 19, 1983

Mam usually puts my tea in the oven if I'm out late. She's mad so she didn't do that tonight. I don't care. I made a bacon butty.
I wonder if the royals eat bacon? I'm sure the queen does, and if she doesn't I'll bet the corgis do.
Bingo with the girls tomorrow night. Hope Gill behaves. Mr Taylor said if he has to speak to her one more time, she's banned.
Book of the week: My Darling Lover
Honeymoon fund: £78.20

CHAPTER 5

WEDNESDAY NIGHT BINGO WITH THE GIRLS WAS USUALLY A FUN night out. A hundred people crammed into the town hall at 7PM sharp to see Betty Shepherd draw numbered ping-pong balls out of a wire barrel.

Despite the fact that she already had a voice like a foghorn, Mr Taylor, the bingo boss, came up with the bright idea of arming her with a microphone. When amplified, Mrs Shepherd could probably be heard in Liverpool.

Bingo was serious business. Giggling or talking while the numbers were being drawn was enough to get you lynched, and we were the worst offenders.

Charlene never broke bingo rules. If anything, she enforced them. We'd only been seated a few minutes when she started laying down the law.

"Just be quiet and play." She pointed her lucky pink bingo dabber pen at Gill. "If you can't keep up, I'll help you."

"Shut up, yer mad cow," snapped Gill. "I can count."

Math skills weren't the issue. Bad behaviour was. Gill was notoriously disruptive and too easily riled, but she wasn't totally out of control. Getting kicked out tonight wasn't an option. There was a hundred quid main prize up for grabs and Gill wanted to win it as much as everybody else in the room.

~

NONE OF US EVEN CAME CLOSE TO WINNING THAT NIGHT, BUT we had a good laugh. It was impossible not to giggle when Mrs Shepherd called out "Dirty Gertie, number thirty." And when the old lady sitting next to Charlene jumped out of her wheelchair to shout bingo and claim her prize, we completely lost the plot.

"Nice one, missus," praised Gill.

Mr Taylor approached and handed the lady her prize money. "Congratulations, love," he said. "It's good to see a regular have a win."

"We're here every week too," Gill interjected. "When are we going to have a win?"

Mr Taylor pointed his finger at her. "Behave yourself," he warned.

Unwilling to give him reason to follow through with his weekly threat of banning her, she didn't answer back. In fact, Gill didn't say much for a while. We were half way to the bus stop before she spoke again. "What would you do with a hundred quid?"

Charlene had obviously put some thought into it. "I'd go on tour with Duran Duran," she answered in a flash.

I wasn't sure why she needed a hundred pounds to do it, but I was impressed by her answer.

Gill wasn't buying it for a second. "What for?" she asked. "You wouldn't know what to do with Simon Le Bon."

Even Charlene's wicked giggle was demure. "I'd figure it out eventually."

The pointless conversation continued all the way to the

bus stop. Gill revealed that she'd bet it all on the horses. "Double or nothing," she exclaimed.

"Wouldn't you be worried about losing it?" asked Charl.

"Had nowt to begin with, right?" Gill shrugged. "You've got to take a chance in life some time."

"I'll remember that next time Simon Le Bon rings me," replied Charlene displaying smart-arse wit that I didn't know she had.

Still laughing, Gill turned to me. "And what about you, princess? What would you do with it?"

I didn't get a chance to answer her. The bus pulled up and we staggered aboard like a group of giggly drunks, which was ironic considering we hadn't had a drop all night. The bus was nearly empty and spirits were high, but all that changed the second we caught sight of the girl sprawled out along the back seat smoking a cigarette. I'd never liked Sharon Smedley. When we were kids, she was a vicious little brute who liked to pull hair and kick people. Now we were grown, not much had changed.

Sharon cut a menacing form. Her black tracksuit was practically her uniform, and the harsh look was topped off with rows of silver hoop earrings and a fierce mono-brow.

Keeping a safe distance wasn't going to save us. The only thing she enjoyed more than her filthy Benson & Hedges addiction was her even filthier habit of winding Gill up. Sharon sat up, giving us her full attention. "Big night out at bingo?" she taunted.

We knew that bingo wasn't a hip pastime for twenty-year-old women. That's why we loved it so much.

"Ignore her," murmured Charlene.

That wasn't going to happen. Gill turned around. "Big night out on the bus, Sharon?" she fired back.

The dirty cow stubbed her smoke out on the floor. "I've been for a night out in Stretford," she explained, directing her comment at me. "Mandy was there," she added with a sly grin.

Mandy Brewer was even dirtier than Sharon. She had a penchant for off the shoulder crop tops and liked to tease her blonde hair to within an inch of its life. She also had a fondness for other people's boyfriends, which is why the next words out of Sharon's mouth made me feel ill.

"Andrew was there too, Fiona," she said. "Getting dead close with Mandy over a pint."

Ever protective, Gill jumped out of her seat, probably with the intent of collaring her. I wasn't going to let it get that far. Sharon was beastly, and Gill didn't stand a chance. "Stop it," I demanded, pulling her back down beside me. "She's just trying to wind us up."

The bus crawled to a stop and Sharon rose to her feet. "You might want to ask him what he's been up to." She squeezed down the narrow aisle to get to the door. "Andy's been a bad, bad lad," she gibed.

"Are you getting off or not?" called the driver.

Sharon stepped off the bus and continued her taunts from the footpath. "Mandy and Andy sitting in a tree," she sang. "K-I-S-I-N-G."

In the biggest surprise of the night, Charlene slid her window open. As the bus pulled away, she hurled a parting shot at Sharon. "You spelt it wrong, dozy bitch!"

DIARY OF FIONA BLACK

WEDNESDAY JULY 20, 1983

*Andrew's been to Stretford twice this week and I want to
know why.*
Tomorrow I'm going to ask him.
Mandy Brewer is a slapper.
Finished reading 'My Darling Lover'.
The ending was stupid.
<u>*Book of the week:*</u> *A Recipe For Romance*
<u>*Honeymoon fund:*</u> *£76.00*

CHAPTER 6

Andrew lives with his father, Dennis, in a flat above the local chippy. For that reason alone, I hate visiting. The whole place stinks of cooking oil, and it's at its worst in summer, but nothing was going to deter me from going there today. After our run in with Sharon, I wanted answers.

Andrew met me at the door, quickly greeting me with a kiss. "Alright, lass?"

I wasn't sure, but I answered with a smile. "Yeah, I just want to talk to you about something."

He nudged me out of the way and closed the door. "Not more wedding talk, Fi." He groaned. "You know I don't care about that stuff."

"How about Mandy Brewer?" I asked. "Do you care about her?"

The flash of panic that glinted in his blue eyes was brief, but I saw it. "No," he replied, outraged. "Why would I?"

"I saw Sharon on the bus last night," I said flatly. "She told me you were hanging out with Mandy in Stretford."

Andrew took a step closer, cautiously weaving his arm around my waist. "Trevor has the hots for her," he quietly explained. "I was just there as his wingman." He kissed my cheek. "You believe me, don't you?"

More than anything in the world, I wanted to. But doubt was gnawing at me so I dodged the question. "I don't want you anywhere near her, Andrew," I demanded. "She's no good."

"Alright," he agreed. "I'll steer clear of her."

I could feel the tension spreading across my chest, but Andrew was his usual unaffected self. As much as I wanted to continue laying down the law, the conversation was over because he'd left me with nowhere to go.

"I'll make you a brew," he offered. "And then I want to show you something special."

I wasn't in the mood for tea, but coming from Andrew, the gesture was too grand to refuse. "Thank you." I smoothed down the back of my skirt and sat down on the settee. "What do you want to show me?"

Already in the kitchen, he called out to me. "You'll have to wait and see."

I knew better than to get my hopes up, and I was right to keep my excitement in check. Andrew's idea of something special was anything but. When he returned to the room, he handed me a cup of tea and pointed to a black box on the floor near the TV stand.

"It's an Atari game station," he explained. "We can play arcade games at home now." The excitement in his voice was unfathomable. "It's dead technical. I've wanted one for ages."

"Where did you get it from?" I asked.

"Trevor knows a bloke," he said vaguely. "He hangs out at the Gloucester Arms. He got me a good deal."

I set my tea down on the coffee table. "Bloody Trevor," I grumbled.

Andrew flopped down beside me. "Don't be like that, lass," he said, patting my knee. "It was a steal at eighty quid."

"Eighty flippin' quid?" The words came out in an angry squeak. "We're supposed to be saving our money!"

Andrew took my hand, probably to lessen the risk of me beating him to a pulp. "That doesn't mean we can't treat ourselves occasionally, Fiona," he said. "While we still can."

I snatched my hand free. "What's that supposed to mean?"

"Well, once we're married it's all over, right?" he asked. "We'll have to start saving for a house of our own, and then kids will come along. There won't be money for treats."

The picture he painted was bleak, and by the sound of it, he was already mourning the loss of his freedom and youth.

"Are you sure you want to marry me?" My eyes narrowed, perhaps bracing for a painful answer. "It's not too late to change your mind."

That was a lie. Every last detail of the wedding had been finalised. Backing out now would break my heart and embarrass both of our families beyond measure.

Andrew dropped to his knees in front of me, taking both of my hands in his. "We're going to get married, Fi," he insisted. "And it's going to be a grand wedding, just like you want."

"It's not just about the wedding," I told him. "You have to think long term. We're going to be married for the rest of our lives. You understand that, don't you?"

He smiled impishly, a grin that made adult conversation practically impossible. "It's going to be ace."

The juvenile response summed up Andrew Pidgeon to a T. As much as I tried to convince myself that he was a grown man who was ready for the commitment we were about to jump headlong into; he was a lad and probably always would be.

DIARY OF FIONA BLACK

THURSDAY JULY 21, 1983

Andrew hardly spoke to me all night. Hopefully the novelty of playing arcade games on the TV wears off soon. If not, he's going to end up with square eyes.

I wonder if Prince Charles has an Atari.

Probably not.

I'm sure he's much too sensible to fork out £80 on a passing fad.

I spent the night reading an old copy of Women's Own that I found stuffed between the sofa cushions and then walked home. Two cats followed me. I'm sure it's because I smelt like fish and chips.

Book of the week: A Recipe for Romance

Honeymoon Fund: £76.00

EVERY NOW AND THEN I STUMBLE ACROSS A BOOK THAT DOES my head in. It's hard to concentrate on anything else, and it drives my mother spare.

"Put the blasted book down and do something productive," she scolded.

I lowered my book and took a long look around the busy shop floor. Reality wasn't looking too special at that point. Two ladies were quibbling over the last set of daisy print sheets in stock and Mrs Wimbush was sizing up crocheting needles while her long-suffering husband waited outside.

Hanging out inside the pages of *A Recipe for Romance* seemed like a much better idea. I was completely taken by the story of a tall, dark and handsome restaurateur from New York. When the girl of his dreams walked in off the street and fell in love with his food, he fell in love with her. It was instant, crushing and left him feeling euphoric and incapable of lucid thoughts.

Those were his words, not mine. The only time I ever felt that was after a skinful of Green Totty cider.

"Do you think men like this really exist, Mam?" I waved the book at her.

"Men like what?" she asked, dumping a bolt of red seersucker down on the counter.

I lifted the dog-eared corner of the page and read out loud. "When he glanced at her and smiled, a magical waterfall of sensations flooded her heart with invigorating delight."

My mother chuckled heartily. "Sounds like a medical condition," she teased. "She should see a doctor."

"Be serious," I whined. "That kind of love must be real if people write about it."

"Total fiction, my girl," she said sternly. "And if it was real, it's not likely to be found in downtown Denton."

"You're right," I agreed with a heavy sigh.

Mam grabbed the end of the roll of fabric and spread it across the counter. "You have Andrew," she reminded me. "He's all you'll ever need – a hardworking man who's good to you."

After measuring the fabric, she instructed me to cut it. "Just once, Mam," I muttered, slicing the razor sharp scissors through the fabric. "I just want to know what it feels like."

She tapped the side of her temple. "Get your head out of the clouds and be thankful for what you have."

I HAD PLENTY TO BE THANKFUL FOR, AND LATER THAT afternoon, I was most thankful for my ace bartering skills. In exchange for babysitting Becky Cox's ratbag kids four Saturdays in a row, she agreed to style my hair.

Finally, the day had come. Charlene agreed to come with me for moral support. No one doubted Becky's hairdressing skills, but she was pushy and rarely followed her customer's instructions. When Gill last visited her salon, she had grand ideas of a gorgeous Princess Di bob. Unfortunately, Becky didn't share her vision. After chopping, teasing and dyeing her hair to death, poor Gill was left looking more like Rod Stewart after a hard night on the town.

Months later, she was still threatening to firebomb the salon so Charlene and I were going it alone.

There are heaps of salons in Denton, but none as classy as Becky's. It had a faux marble linoleum floor, macramé plant holders hanging from the ceiling, and bright vanity lighting around the mirrors. Even Charlene was impressed.

"This is a bit flash, isn't it?" she asked.

Becky was a bit flash too. Her pinstriped denim jumpsuit was straight out of the pages of a fashion mag. She wheeled her plastic cart of tools and brushes over to the mirrors and told us to take a seat.

"So what did you have in mind?" she asked, raking her fingers through my hair from behind.

"Something ace," I told her. "We're hitting the town tonight."

"Oooh," she crowed. "Somewhere special?"

I smiled but didn't answer. Flamingo Harry's could hardly be described as special, but it was the only place to be on a Friday night. We could dance until our legs gave way and make the most of happy hour, which confusingly ran from six until nine.

The problem was, we weren't the only ones who enjoyed the music and cheap drinks. The rest of the Denton crew made the most of it too, including Mandy Brewer and her henchman, Sharon.

"The club should be bursting tonight," said Charlene. "I heard they're having a live band."

I grinned at her through the mirror. "Duran Duran?"

"At Flamingo Harry's?" she choked. "I flippin' doubt it."

"You need colour," interjected Becky. "Then we'll put it up – maybe a French roll with some curls on top." She twisted my long hair and piled it on top of my head.

Nerves got the better of me then as flashbacks of Gill's Rod Stewart do flooded my mind. "What colour?" I asked. "Nothing crazy."

Becky grabbed a colour chart from her trolley and dropped it onto my lap. "Pick one," she said. "A lovely burgundy tint would suit you."

"Fi, you can't," hissed Charlene from the corner of her mouth. "Your mam will kill you."

She was right. Despite the tight budget, I was expected to do my mother proud as an elegant and sophisticated bride, which meant a hip dye job would never fly. The only burgundy at my wedding would be the cheap box wine.

"How about this one?" I asked, pointing at a shade of brown that was very similar to my natural colour. "Chestnut Victory."

Becky snatched the colour chart. "Not much of a flippin' victory if you ask me," she replied. "But it's your head."

～

Becky Cox could talk the hind leg off a donkey. The woman was a waif – so tiny that her chic denim jumpsuit might well have come from the Marks and Spencer's children's catalogue. Too curious for my own good, I once asked her how she stayed so thin.

"Simple," she replied with a casual shrug. "I haven't had a meal since 1978."

As small as she was, her mouth was huge. She talked as she worked, barely pausing for breath as she brought us up to speed on the local gossip. I didn't know most of the people she was talking about, but it didn't make it any less fascinating.

"I heard that Bruce was shagging the bird from the off-license weeks ago," she said, roughly dabbing at my scalp with the dye-laden brush. "But Elaine refused to believe it." She smirked at me through the mirror. "She does now, though."

"What changed her mind?" asked Charlene.

"A nasty case of the clap," Becky revealed with a giggle. "The fire in her heart is out, but her lady parts are still burning."

I cracked up laughing, but poor Charlene looked mortified. "Oh dear," she mumbled.

The stories only got more sordid from that point on. By the time the dye was rinsed from my hair, we had dirt on half the town. As Becky led me back to my chair from the sink, she swore us both to secrecy. "You mustn't repeat a word," she warned. "I don't want people thinking I'm a gossip."

Becky Cox wasn't merely a gossip. She was an educator. The circle that I moved in was insular and tame – a world away from the likes of Elaine and her itchy crotch. It highlighted just how naïve and sheltered we were, and that wasn't necessarily a good thing.

Another thing that wasn't particularly good was Becky's listening skills. As soon as I caught a glimpse of my wet hair in the mirror, I knew she'd ignored my Chestnut Victory request.

"Flippin' hellfire," gasped Charlene.

For her, it was a crass outburst, but nothing compared with the slew of curse words that tumbled out of my mouth.

My mother was going to murder me.

Long, wet, claret coloured strands flew in every direction as Becky towelled my hair. "Grape Delight," she announced. "Much more lively than boring old brown."

"I'm getting married in a few weeks, Becky!" I shrieked. "You have to change it back before my mam sees it."

Completely ignoring my desperate demand, she reached for the hairdryer. "It's edgy," she insisted. "Like a popstar."

Nothing could be heard over the sound of the roaring hairdryer so the next ten minutes were spent staring helplessly at my reflection, trying to imagine how I'd look as a popstar bride.

Hideous, I concluded.

Based on the fact that she could barely look at me, Charlene obviously agreed. Words weren't forthcoming either. We'd long escaped the salon and almost made it to the bus stop before she finally spoke.

"At least you don't look like Rod Stewart."

I grinded to a halt and turned to face her. "What *do* I look like, Charlene?"

"Awful." Her shoulders lifted – and stayed there. "But we'll sort it. Gill will know what to do."

"And if she doesn't?" I asked.

"Run away to London," Charlene suggested. "Pierce your ears with safety pins and join the punk scene." Ever the optimist, she followed up with a dreamy sigh. "London would be so exciting," she breathed.

I almost laughed at the absurdity. "My hair is as red as a radish and my wedding is going to be ruined because of it," I reminded her. "I don't need any more excitement."

~

SOMEHOW, WE MADE IT ALL THE WAY TO CHARLENE'S HOUSE without running into anyone we knew. The shock of seeing my garish new do was reserved entirely for Gill, who showed up at a little after six.

"Bloody hell, Fi," she gasped. "That's a bit out there, isn't it?"

"Shush," warned Charlene, pushing her bedroom door closed. "Keep your voice down."

I didn't think there was any need to speak quietly. The four million stuffed animals taking up space in her bedroom had to provide soundproofing.

"How do we fix it?" I asked.

Gill shrugged. "Shave it off?"

"That's the best you've got?"

"I actually quite like it," she replied, raising her arm to deflect the Smurf I'd just hurled at her. "It's dead contemporary."

I wasn't a fan of contemporary. I was a royalist who favoured tradition and elegance. I had a Mel Lazar clutch bag to prove it for crying out loud.

I slumped down on the edge of the bed and put my hands to my face. "It's hopeless."

"It'll be okay, Fi," soothed Charlene.

Gill's attempt at placating me was a little less orthodox, but far more effective. She reached into her bag and pulled out a bottle of Green Totty Cider.

"Get this into yer." The bottle hissed as she twisted the lid. "You'll feel better in no time."

We passed the Totty around until the bottle was empty, and like magic, I did begin to feel better.

"Sod my hair," I grumbled. "Let's go to Flamingo Harry's and dance."

DIARY OF FIONA BLACK

FRIDAY JULY 22, 1983

Maybe the dull lighting in the club worked in my favour.
One bloke at the bar said my new do reminded him of the pretty
girl from Bucks Fizz. I was quite chuffed until Charlene reminded
me that they're both blonde.
It was all downhill from there.
Trevor spent the whole night showing off his break dancing moves.
The DJ came over the mic and called him talented. Gill called him
a wanker, which was closer to the mark.
He looked like a skinny giraffe in tight pants having a seizure.
Andrew never showed up at all. Worse than that, Mandy Brewer
was a no-show too.
Book of The Week: A Recipe for Romance
Honeymoon fund: £69.00

CHAPTER 8

Gill and I both spent the night at Charlene's. Bedding down on a half inflated air mattress and a dozen stuffed teddy bears is never comfortable, but it was a darn sight less painful than dealing with my mother.

Charlene woke first, and had used the time alone to research. She waved a magazine at me. "I'm glad you're awake." Her tone was much too chipper for someone who'd consumed a whole jug of Blue Lagoon cocktails by herself the night before. "I found an article in Glam Girl. It says laundry powder will strip the colour from your hair."

I wasn't convinced, but Gill piped up in agreement. "You need the good stuff, though," she said mid yawn. "Cheap-arse Daz won't cut it, you need Persil."

Charlene threw back the covers and leapt out of bed. "We use Persil!"

"Of course you do," mumbled Gill. "Only the best for Lady Charlene."

"Shut up, Gill," snapped Charlene. "Your mam uses Persil too."

It was an argument that I wasn't prepared to weigh in on.

My head was pounding. "I just want to get it sorted," I said, struggling to sit up. "Then I'm going home."

Charlene slipped out of the room, presumably to raid her mother's laundry supplies. I made a start on folding up the bedding, but Gill was more intent on mischief. She threw open the wardrobe doors and made a grab for the empty cider bottle that Charlene had hidden the night before. "Besides the hair, what's wrong?" she asked.

I was almost impressed that she noticed I was out of sorts. Gill wasn't renowned for her caring and sensitive side. She was more of a crack-skulls-and-apologise-later kind of gal.

"Andrew never showed up last night," I muttered. "Where do you suppose he was?"

Setting her sights on a dopey looking plush panda sitting on the bookshelf, Gill wrapped its paws around the cider bottle. "Do you want me to lie and make you feel better or do you want the truth?"

The panda slumped to the side, but I remained steady. "The truth," I said bravely.

"I think he was probably up to no good," she said, straightening the toy up. "I've never known him to miss Friday night happy hour before."

Nor had I, and Mandy Brewer certainly never missed an opportunity to dance all night and drink on the cheap.

"Do you think he's stepping out on me, Gill?"

She pointed at the defiled panda. "If it walks like a drunk panda, and talks like a drunk panda, it's a drunk panda."

"Very insightful, thank you," I grumbled.

"Look," she continued, slightly penitently. "I think you should at least find out one way or another before you follow the numbskull down the aisle."

"I'm scared to find out," I admitted. "I'd be so humiliated if I had to call it all off."

"Listen to yourself, Fi," she urged. "You're more worried about losing your wedding day than your groom."

Gill's no-nonsense opinions were notoriously hard to listen to, usually because she was right. I'd spent months planning the perfect wedding day, but it had always been a solo pursuit. Andrew Pidgeon didn't give a damn about any of it, and maybe that meant he didn't give a damn about the marriage either.

~

ACCORDING TO GLAM GIRL MAGAZINE, THE ANSWER TO MY hair problems was a thick paste made of washing powder and water.

But Glam Magazine was shaping up to be a crock.

An hour later, my hair felt like wet straw and was still a hideous shade of claret. On the plus side, I smelled like freshly washed sheets.

"I'm destined to be a ginger forever," I wailed, studying my reflection in the dressing table mirror.

Charlene was undeterred. She sat down on her bed and re-read the article, looking for further instruction. "It says you might have to repeat the process three or four times."

Gill snatched the magazine from her grasp. "She won't have any flippin' hair left at this rate," she grumbled. "You should leave it alone for a few days, Fi."

As much as it pained me, I tended to agree. Being a stop-light redhead is one thing, but being bald would be a whole new level of horror.

"I'll try it again tomorrow," I said wanly. "Thanks for trying."

Gill grinned at me through the mirror. "We're always here for you, Ginge."

Charlene let out a squeal that made me jump, but it had

nothing to do with Gill's wise crack. "What have you done to my panda?" She ripped the cider bottle from its grasp and thrust it at Gill. "I didn't invite you over here to besmirch my animals."

I tried not to laugh but it was impossible. Gill didn't even try. She howled with laughter. "Besmirched?" she asked, mid cackle. "Who even says that?"

"I bet Princess Di does," I replied.

"Yes," agreed Charlene. "So there."

"Bloody ancient royalists." Gill handed the cider back to Charlene. "In case you haven't noticed, it's 1983. Get with the times."

❧

MY MAM DOESN'T USE PERSIL. SHE DOESN'T USE TACT OR discretion either.

"Bleedin' hellfire, Fiona!" She screamed. "What have you done?"

Showing up at the shop probably wasn't the best idea, but I figured there would be safety in numbers.

Clearly, I was wrong.

She didn't give a damn about making a scene in front of her customers. When one quietly asked her to calm down, Mam turned on her in an instant. "You bloody calm down, Vera!" she snapped. "It's not your daughter who's traipsing around town looking like a dog's dinner."

That wasn't entirely true. Vera Smedley was Sharon's mother. More often than not, her daughter traipsed around town looking like the dog that ate the dog's dinner.

"It's just hair, Mam," I said flatly.

With an expression of pure thunder, she ordered me out of the shop. "I'll deal with you later."

"There's nothing to deal with." I spoke strongly, mainly for Vera's benefit. "I'm a ginger now."

I was a twenty-year-old woman on the verge of getting married. Any plan my mam had of banishing me to my room and giving me a good hiding wasn't likely to happen, but that didn't mean I wasn't scared of her.

Backchat wasn't my forte so the loud bang I heard as I trudged toward the door could've been her collapsing to the floor, but I didn't look back and check. I headed straight home, grabbed a box of washing powder and locked myself in the bathroom.

~

THERE'S MERIT IN BEING PERSISTENT. IGNORING THE THREAT of baldness, I slapped another round of washing powder paste on my head, left it on as long as I could stand and was rewarded with a good result. Dark burgundy locks weren't exactly ideal, but it was acceptable.

Mam wasn't so easily pacified. When I finally opened the bathroom door, she was standing in the hall waiting for me. "I'll book you in at Becky Cox's tomorrow," she snapped. "She'll get it sorted in no time."

I inched past her and let out a growl. "Becky's the one who dyed it, Mam."

She was hot on my heels as I took the few short steps across the hall to my bedroom. "I'll bloody strangle her!"

I grabbed the small mirror off my dressing table and checked my reflection for the umpteenth time. "It's not too bad now," I replied, fluffing my hair.

Mam sat down on the edge of my bed. "It's not suitable for a bride," she insisted. "You look like a trollop."

The name calling didn't reduce me to tears. It was the mention of the wedding that made me unravel. My poor mother didn't know what to make of it. She reached for my hand and pulled me close, awkwardly hugging my head as I sat beside her on the bed.

"What on earth is wrong?" she asked quietly.

I didn't know where to start. Bringing her up to speed with a disjointed ramble was the best I could do.

"Don't believe everything you hear," she uttered. "Andrew would never be unfaithful."

"But what if it's true, Mam?"

She smoothed her hand through my tortured hair. "You're a Black, my girl," she said with reverence. "We're dignified in times of trouble. You hold your head high and carry on."

"I'd be gutted if I have to call the wedding off," I cried.

"You'll do no such thing." Her voice was quiet but stern. "Weather the storm, Fiona. No matter what happens."

As horrified as I was by her attitude, I wasn't surprised. To my mother, appearances are everything.

"I can't go through with it if – "

"Go and wash your face," she said, cutting me off. "You'll feel much better."

The conversation was over, but at least I knew where I stood. The invitations had gone out and the flowers had been ordered. Despite the fact that my fiancé might be a cheating scumbag, a deal is a deal. I was getting married whether I wanted to or not.

DIARY OF FIONA BLACK

SATURDAY JULY 23, 1983

Charles and Diana are touring Canada. It was the leading story on the news tonight.
Charles didn't crack a smile, but I could tell he was happy. How could he not be? The queen lent him the royal yacht.
Di looked dead lovely, dressed in yellow from head to toe.
Imagine how ace her life must be!
True love, riches and a tiara for every day of the week.
I'd be happy with true love and one tiara but most days, both seem out of reach.
<u>Book of the week:</u> A Recipe for Romance
<u>Honeymoon Fund:</u> £63.00

CHAPTER 9

PRIVATE PHONE CALLS ARE PRACTICALLY IMPOSSIBLE IN OUR tiny flat, especially if they're taking place between nine and ten on a Saturday night when Mam is watching Dynasty. She refused to leave the room when Andrew called so the conversation was short.

He made no apology for being a no-show the night before, nor did he offer an explanation. Instead, he offered to take me out to lunch the next day. It wasn't likely to be a grand affair, but I still wanted to look nice.

When I caught sight of myself in the mirror, I realised that meant I needed to rethink my choice of outfit. My favourite green dress clashed horribly with my hair, making me look like a dead ringer for a Christmas elf. Thankfully, my second favourite dress looked much less festive. I teamed it with a wide silver belt, slipped on some strappy sandals and headed out the door.

Andrew was already waiting, revving the engine of the junky Cortina to keep it running. When I slipped into the passenger seat he greeted me with wide eyes and a look of alarm.

I held off pulling the door closed. If the next words out of his mouth were as grave as his expression, I was ready to leg it back to the house.

"What happened to your hair?" he asked, aghast.

I wound my super chic side pony tail around my hand. "I dyed it," I uttered. "Do you like it?"

"No," he replied. "Was it supposed to turn out like that?"

"Not really," I replied coolly. "But you can't always get what you want, can you?"

～

THE BRIDGE END café wasn't exactly the flashiest place in town. It was nowhere near a bridge either. It was located on a busy street right in the middle of the shopping precinct.

It had been there forever, and its longevity was reflected by the tired décor. The gingham tablecloths were mismatched and ratty, the vinyl floor tiles were lifting and the lace curtains were discoloured, but the food was good. It was also cheap, which explained why it was one of our favourite haunts.

Before we even sat down, Andrew ordered two Cokes. I chose a spot near the window, discreetly brushed some crumbs off the table and gave the cutlery a quick wipe with a serviette.

"This is posh," Andrew said, squaring up the small vase in the centre of the table.

A dusty plastic carnation could never be posh, but I agreed with him anyway. "Flamingo Harry's was good the other night," I said, changing the subject. "They had a live band."

His smile was strained. "I'm sorry I missed it."

"Where were you?"

"Playing my Atari, mostly," he replied. "I got up to level eight. It's dead addictive."

Feigning apathy, I reached for a menu. "By yourself?" I quizzed. "Mandy wasn't there either."

Andrew let out a pissed off groan. "Not this again, Fiona," he complained. "I told you before, I've had nowt to do with Mandy bleedin' Brewer."

My first instinct was to apologise for jumping to conclusions, but I managed to hold back. It didn't matter whether I'd lost out to arcade games or another woman, he'd still blown me off.

"You could've called," I mumbled.

Andrew's shoulders slumped. "I just needed some time away, Fi," he confessed.

"From me?"

I had to wait for an answer. An unenthusiastic waitress made her way over to our table, scuffing her feet as she walked. "Ready to order?" she asked, offloading two bottles of Coke onto the table.

"Not yet." Andrew's eyes never left mine. "Give us a minute."

She moseyed away without another word paving the way for the tense conversation to continue.

"You're doing my head in," he told me. "I'm sick of wedding talk all the time."

The annoyance I felt was overshadowed by confusion. I purposefully kept the wedding talk to a minimum around Andrew. He had no interest in bridesmaid dresses or bouquet designs so sharing those details with him would have been an aggravating waste of breath.

Then it hit me.

The subject of the wedding wasn't the irritant. Marriage was the topic of conversation that had sent him running. I hounded him every chance I got, desperately seeking assurance that he was on board with our plans.

I wanted a loving marriage, a pretty home and a handful of kids. It was a set of goals that made Gill and other like-minded modern women cringe, but they were my dreams and they were valid.

"We have to want the same things," I said for the umpteenth time. "It's important."

Andrew reached for my hand and gave my fingers a light squeeze. "You're like a broken record. Just tone it down a notch, Fi."

I pulled away, but he didn't seem to notice. He picked up a menu and called out to the waitress.

I used the time it took for her to scuff her way over to pull myself together, refusing to show the hurt I was feeling.

She pulled a notebook out of the pocket of her apron. "What'll it be?"

"Two chips and eggs," replied Andrew ordering for both of us.

"I don't want chips and eggs," I protested.

He frowned. "But that's what you always order."

"Maybe it's time I tried something new."

Andrew picked up the menu and studied it again. "Maybe we should both try something new."

Clearly, we weren't talking about chips and eggs any more but I didn't ask for clarification. Marrying this Atari addicted man-child who may or may not be cheating on me would be the biggest mistake of my short life, but I took my mother's advice and battened down to weather the storm.

DIARY OF FIONA BLACK

SUNDAY JULY 24, 1983

I hate it when he orders food for me.
I hate the ugly blue jacket he always wears.
I hate his ugly car.
His friends are idiots.
<u>Book of the week:</u> A Recipe for Romance
<u>Honeymoon Fund:</u> £63.00

WITH JUST A FEW WEEKS TO GO BEFORE THE WEDDING, MY LIFE was in shambles. Andrew had basically checked out. I hadn't heard from him in two days, and if I was being honest, I'd admit that I didn't really care.

Cleaning house for Mrs Crichton-Percy was fast becoming the highlight of my week.

The lady of the manor met me at the door with a wide smile and a vague set of instructions. "Just flitter around and give things a good spruce." She handed me a bucket of cleaning supplies. "You can start in the bedrooms."

I dutifully followed her upstairs, dusting a cloth along the rail of the bannister as I went.

"My friend Judith is here." She spoke as if I knew who Judith was. "We're sorting through clothes to sell at the charity auction."

Philanthropic ventures seemed to be a common pastime for privileged women like Mrs Crichton-Percy. Charlene's mother was also a fixture on the charity scene.

"Do you like doing charity work?" I asked, taking the last step up onto the landing.

"It serves a purpose." She turned back, smiling wryly. "It's a good way of keeping designer gowns out of thrift shops."

I was secretly appalled, but probably just looked confused. I'd come to know Mrs Crichton-Percy as a generous person; constantly overpaying me and gifting me lovely things. But she was showing a new side that I wasn't sure I liked.

I gave the bucket a shake. "I should make a start."

Before she could reply, a posh voice called out from the bedroom. "Are these the best coat hangers you've got, darling?" she asked. "They're frightfully tatty."

I would've told her to sod off, but Mrs Crichton-Percy turned and dashed into the bedroom as if she'd been beckoned by the queen herself. I stayed put, electing to eavesdrop from the doorway.

"I have some lovely crocheted hangers," she offered.

The woman let out a strange groan. "Crochet – how delightful."

She didn't mean it, and Mrs Crichton-Percy knew it. Within seconds, she volunteered to buy some new ones. "Perhaps padded velvet?"

I don't know what possessed me to round the doorway and put my two cents in, but I did it. "My mam sells velvet hangers in her shop," I volunteered. "They're dead lovely."

When Judith spun around to face me, the first thing I noticed was her earrings. The huge glittery baubles looked heavy as heck. Perhaps that explained her stiff posture.

"And who might you be, darling?" she asked, looking me up and down.

"Nobody." I raised the bucket of cleaning supplies. "I'm just here to clean."

Her heavily made up eyes bored right through me. "The notion of a pretty young girl introducing herself as a nobody is troubling. Don't ever do it again."

Clearly, the woman was rude, but she was also fascinating and had gorgeous shoes so I corrected the faux pas by telling her my name.

"Her mother owns the haberdashery shop in Denton," added Mrs Crichton-Percy.

The unnecessary footnote was annoying, and it riled Judith too. "I didn't ask about her mother," she snapped.

Perhaps feeling suitably chastised, Mrs Crichton-Percy quickly changed the subject. "I think it's time for a spot of tea."

"That's a lovely idea, darling," praised Judith. "Fiona can join us."

Judging by her sucking-lemon expression, that wasn't my boss' plan. "Wonderful," she muttered, heading for the door.

Within seconds of being alone in the room, Judith dropped the prickly attitude. "I cannot stand her," she whispered.

"Why?" I whispered back.

Her ensuing smile was as harsh as her ruby lipstick. "Nina Crichton-Percy simply tries too hard." She scooped a long blue dress off the bed and held it up. "New with tags," she noted. "The woman is so determined to pack a punch on the charity scene that she resorts to donating new gowns."

It might've been the most beautiful dress in the world, but I paid no attention to it. My focus was solely on the three hundred quid price tag dangling from the sleeve.

"What a waste," I muttered, mainly to myself.

"Frivolous to say the least." Judith dropped the dress onto the bed in a messy heap. "But it's not her fault. Money can't buy class."

Thanks to Judith's loose but cutting tongue, I learned a lot about the inner workings of high society over the next few minutes – and alarmingly, Mrs Crichton-Percy didn't pass muster.

"She'll never be part of the fold," she said pityingly. "But enough about New-Money-Nina. I want to know more about you." Judith turned back to face me, looking me up and down again. "Why are you housecleaning in Bramhall?"

"Because I'm No-Money-Fiona," I cheekily replied. "I need this job."

"I don't believe that's the only reason, darling," she accused. "I think you're a curious girl."

She was right. I was curious about a million things. For example, why did she tack the word 'darling' onto the end of every sentence? And how the heck did she manage to glue her false lashes on so straight? The few times I had tried had ended in disaster.

Those were the sorts of things I wondered about when in the company of high society women. I studied them in the same way I pored over fashion magazines, and Judith had called me out on it.

"I like to see how the other half lives," I confessed.

"Do you think the grass is greener on this side of the fence, Fiona?"

"Yes," I replied simply. My life was a slippery slope of disappointment and uncertainty, but I still believed in the fairy-tale ending. "One day I'm going to have the greenest grass of all."

It sounded strong and plausible only for a second, and then Mrs Crichton-Percy killed it. The cups on the tray rattled beneath her grasp as she cackled her way into the room. "You're marrying an apprentice bricklayer, Fiona," she said. "Perhaps you should've set your sights on a landscaper instead."

Before embarrassment could take hold, Judith swooped in. "You were right about the hangers, Nina." She pointed at the dresses laid out on the bed. "Velvet would be suitable. We'll need at least twenty."

"Now?" Mrs Crichton-Percy's eyes widened. "We have work to do."

"Fiona can help me," Judith suggested. "You run along."

Doing little to disguise her disdain, my boss snatched her handbag off the dresser and headed for the door. It wasn't the half hour drive to Denton that pissed her off. I'd inadvertently muscled in on her playdate, and that would've infuriated anyone.

"Maybe I should get back to the cleaning," I said as soon as she was gone. "She's cross with me."

"Nonsense," Judith scoffed. "She's cross with me."

And from what I could tell, the most glamorous, cutting woman I'd ever met didn't care one iota.

"Are you the leader of your friends?"

The crass question tumbled out of my mouth, but rather than take offense, she threw back her head and laughed.

"The leader?" She giggled. "Explain what you mean, darling."

Desperate to avoid eye contact, I scooped a gown off the bed and clumsily tried folding it. "Well, in my group of friends, Gill is the leader. She's dead smart and tough as nails." She was also crooked as heck, but I left that part out. "Whenever there's drama, she always handles it."

"I don't handle drama, darling," she replied. "I like to nip it in the bud before it takes hold." Judith took the dress from my grasp and laid it back on the bed. "Do you have drama in your life Fiona?"

I dragged my ponytail over my shoulder and picked at the dry ends. "Only my hair colour," I replied half-jokingly. "That was a drama and a half."

"Experimentation is a rite of passage." She smiled brightly. "You'll make a hundred more mistakes along the way, and they won't all be beauty related."

"I'm getting married in a few weeks." The random

comment was delivered in a dismal tone. "That's a mistake I'd like to nip in the bud."

It was a terrible admission to make, but the relief that came with saying it out loud felt wonderful.

"You mustn't go through with it if you're unhappy, darling." Judith sat down on the edge of the bed and patted the empty space beside her. "Call it off at once."

She made backing out of my wedding sound as simple as cancelling a lunch date. I knew differently, and wasted no time in telling her so.

I sat beside her. "My mam will skin me alive."

"Your mother isn't marrying him," she shot back.

"No, but she's been planning the wedding for a long time."

Judith let out a hard, humourless laugh. "Oh, dear girl."

The only thing worse than feeling inferior is feeling pitied. It immediately got my back up. "Andrew's not a bad guy," I defended. "He just doesn't make me giddy."

"Giddy?"

Her confused expression left me wondering if giddy was even a real word.

I leaned, dragging my latest tattered read out of the back pocket of my jeans. As I thumbed through the pages of *A Recipe for Romance*, Judith asked an incredulous question.

"Do you often carry books in your back pocket, darling?"

"Always," I replied. "That's why I love Mills and Boons. They're only thin so they don't make my bum look big."

Finally, her laugh sounded genuine. "Quite."

Without asking permission, I cleared my throat and began to read out loud. "Giddy with lust, Angelica felt a tidal wave of molten lava burn her heart to a cinder."

"Gosh," said Judith. "That's frightfully dramatic."

"Is it real?" My hopeful tone reeked of desperation. "I need it to be real."

"What does your mother say about it?"

My shoulders sagged as I loosened my grip on the book. "She tells me that I need to get my head out of the clouds and start living in the real world."

"I see."

"I'm just a hopeful romantic."

"Hopeless romantic, Fiona," she corrected, patting my knee.

"No, hopeful is the right term," I insisted. "Hopefully I'll get burned by lava one day soon."

"Are we talking about sex now, darling?"

"I don't know. Are we?"

The naïve question highlighted just how clueless I was. I was saving myself for marriage – at least that was the official line – but lately I wondered if I was just saving myself for someone worthy.

Judith looked as confused as I felt. "You mean you've never…"

I shook my head, killing the need for her to finish the awkward question.

"We've fooled around." I tried to sound confident and experienced, but failed. "But I want it to be special."

And the back seat of the Cortina could never be special.

Judith's smile had a rueful tinge. "I'm no expert, darling," she said gently. "But I will tell you this. If there's no spark now, there will never be lava."

I wished my mother could be as frank, but by her own admission, she knew nothing about passion. Her 'lie back and think of England attitude' served her well for ten long years – and then my father left her for a barmaid from the Gloucester Arms and moved to Skegness. As far as I knew, she'd never been with another man since, and that seemed to suit her just fine.

"You need a man who can make your toes curl," added Judith. "Surely you talk about this with your friends."

"None of us are very worldly," I confessed. "The last bloke who tried to kiss Gill ended up with a split lip for his troubles, and Charlene is still saving herself for Simon Le Bon. I guess we still have some growing up to do."

In a motherly move that I wasn't expecting, Judith reached out and tucked a long strand of burgundy hair behind my ear. "You'll get there, darling." She spoke with absolute certainty. "And when you do, you'll see just how green the grass can be."

DIARY OF FIONA BLACK

WEDNESDAY JULY 27, 1983

I met a lady called Judith Wiltshire, and I'm pretty sure she has the whole world worked out. She's dead elegant, very posh and says 'darling' every two seconds.
My life goals are changing.
Get my hair back to a nice shade of normal.
Find a prince who makes my toes curl.
Be like Judith.
I guess that means the wedding is off. How am I going to get out of this one?
Book of the week: Sky High Lovers
Honeymoon Fund: £68.00

CHAPTER 11

BINGO BONANZA IS ONE OF DENTON'S BIGGEST EVENTS OF THE year. People come from far and wide for a chance to win the thousand quid main prize, and Gill, Charlene and I were usually first in the door.

This year's event was sponsored by the local butcher, and Mr Cooper of Cooper's Cuts went all out to make sure it was a grand affair.

We were out to win the money, but Mam was more interested in the raffle prizes that were up for grabs. I was under strict instruction not to come home without a meat tray.

"I'll settle for a few pounds of sausages," she called as I pulled the front door shut.

Winning a meat tray wasn't a given, but the odds were good. Mr Cooper was a generous man, which was evident from the second we walked into the bingo hall. Cardboard lamb chops hung from the ceiling, and the huge cache of meat prizes were artfully displayed on bales of hay near the stage.

"Bleedin' hellfire," muttered Gill.

I thought the blow-up cow near the front door was a nice touch, but she saw fit to punch it as she passed.

"Give over!" Mr Taylor yelled from the far side of the hall. "Any more of that and you're out!"

Gill must've really had her eye on the prize; she apologised and promised to behave.

We took our usual seats by the stage. Charlene spent the next few minutes getting her coloured markers in order and lining them up neatly on the table while Gill and I rifled through our bags looking for loose change.

When Mrs Shepherd wandered past flapping her raffle books in our faces, we snapped up as many as we could afford.

"We're going to win big tonight, girls," shrieked Charlene, neatening the tickets into a pile. "I'm feeling lucky."

I felt lucky too. We were together, we had gallons of Green Totty cider hidden in our handbags and best of all, once the balls started dropping there would be no time for talking.

I didn't know how I was going to break it to them that the wedding was off. Heck, I didn't even know how I was going to tell Andrew.

Thankfully, it was a problem for another day. Mrs Shepherd took the mic and ordered everyone to sit. The hall suddenly became a flurry of activity as people rushed to their chairs, bingo dabbers at the ready.

Sharon Smedley wasn't exactly rushing. She stalked past the back of our chairs at a snail's pace. Never one to pass up an opportunity to rattle her cage, Gill piped up.

"Ace tracksuit, Shaz," she taunted. "Are you flying solo tonight or is Mandy hiding somewhere under all that crushed velvet?"

"Mandy's not here," she sneered.

"Where is she?" asked Charlene. I swung my leg under the

table, trying to silence her with a kick – but I missed and she kept talking. "No one misses Bingo Bonanza."

Sharon's snarky glare was reserved entirely for me. "I could lie and say she's at home if you like," she goaded. "Do you want me to lie, Fiona?"

Gill answered for me. "*I* want you to lie," she snapped. "Preferably in front of oncoming traffic."

The three of us dissolved into a fit of derisive giggles, which wound Sharon up to the point of detonation.

Thankfully Mrs Shepherd intervened, picking up the mic and yelling as if she needed the amplification. "You're the last man standing, Sharon," she barked. "Find a seat."

A low rumbling of laughter filled the packed hall, but we didn't even try to be discreet. We cackled like witches as Sharon skulked away, and when she parked her ample bum on her seat, Mrs Shepherd got the ball rolling by calling the first number. "Knock at the door, twenty-four."

~

SOME BLOKE FROM YORKSHIRE WON THE THOUSAND QUID. THE locals were outraged, but we couldn't have cared less. We were winners in our own right, which made for an interesting walk to the bus stop. I had two frozen chickens in my bag, Gill was cradling a leg of pork like a baby, and Charlene awkwardly held her package at arm's length.

"What do you think it is?" she asked, waving it in Gill's face.

The brown paper parcel was a mystery, but we knew it was meat; blood was leaking through the wrapping.

"Gross!" she yelled, whacking her hand away.

I laughed, partly because it was funny, and partly because I had a skinful of Green Totty. We all did, and were walking incredibly slowly because of it.

It was a little after ten when we finally made it to the bus stop, and after half an hour of waiting, it finally dawned on us that we'd missed the last bus.

Even after pooling our money, we were still a long way short of cab fare.

"We shouldn't have spent it all on raffle tickets," Charlene lamented.

Gill patted her lump of pork. "No regrets, girlies."

"None," I agreed with a tipsy giggle.

The prospect of walking home didn't bother me. It was a fine night and I was with my best friends. As far as I was concerned life didn't get much better, despite Charlene's drunken rambling.

"What's a male ballerina called?" she asked out of the blue. It wasn't a trick question. The girl was deadly serious. "I've always wondered."

"A ballerino," replied Gill, hitching her pork higher on her hip.

After a long moment of thinking things through, Charlene accepted her answer. "I guess that makes sense."

"Unlike you," muttered Gill. "Yer dozy cow."

I laughed until my sides ached, and it was the best kind of pain I'd ever felt. For a moment, I had no worries. I felt free, young and untroubled – and then we turned the corner.

~

I would've recognised Andrew's trashy Cortina anywhere, but I wasn't expecting to see it parked on Darnley Road. It was a long way from home, especially at eleven o'clock at night.

"Maybe it broke down," suggested Charlene.

I was shaking my head before she'd finished the sentence.

"If it breaks, he fixes it," I told her. "The damn car just won't die."

"Fi, you should probably know something." Gill's grave tone sobered me up in an instant. Something terrible was on its way.

"What is it?"

"Mandy Brewer lives here." She motioned with an upward nod. "They moved in a few weeks ago."

I leaned to the side, checking out the modest terraced house behind her. Other than the blue front door, it was fairly nondescript, which was almost odd considering that the shenanigans taking place inside were probably extraordinary.

Strangely, I wasn't feeling upset or angry so I don't know what possessed me to yell Andrew's name. After repeating the obnoxious shriek a few times, the upstairs window finally slid open. A light came on and my cad of a fiancé appeared, flustered and tangled up in the lace curtain. "Fi, it's not what you think," he blundered.

I was certain it was. He was dragging on his T-shirt as he spoke.

"So what is it, Andrew?" I threw my arms wide. "Tea and toast?"

The curtain shifted and he disappeared from view, probably looking to his mistress for answers. I was prepared to give them a minute to get their story straight. Whatever they came up with was bound to be good.

"We should go." Charlene tugged on my sleeve. "Deal with it in the morning."

I shrugged her off, mainly because her hands were covered in bloody meat juice. "No," I grumbled. "I want to deal with it now."

I had no clue how it was going to play out. I expected a rambling monologue laced with apologies, but when Andrew reappeared at the window, his expression confused me. He didn't look contrite and remorseful – he looked determined.

"It's over, Fiona," he coolly stated. "The wedding is off."

I was completely off the hook, which is exactly what I wanted. So why did I feel so blindsided by the announcement? I couldn't think of a single thing to say. Instead of cutting him down with a furious reply, I stood there, slack jawed and silent.

"Nothing is ever good enough for you," he spat. "And I've flippin' had enough."

I couldn't make sense of what was happening. Not only was Andrew unremorseful, he had the gall to be angry with me.

Gill was obviously struggling with the notion too. She took a few steps forward and yelled like only Gill could. "You're the cheater, dickhead!" she reminded him. "You don't get to be pissed."

The loathing between my fiancé and best friend was mutual, and it had been that way since nursery school.

Charlene was a little more tolerant of him, but even she had a limit. "You're a knob, Andrew!" Even her angry tone was sweet. "You'll never do better than Fi!"

When he leaned out the window and replied with a middle finger, something inside me snapped. Andrew wasn't the knob, I was. I'd hitched every hope and dream I'd had since childhood to his wagon – and his wagon was a 1974 Ford Cortina for crying out loud.

Rage was the prime emotion at that point. When I looked across at his pride and joy parked crookedly on the street I lost all control, reached into my bag and grabbed a frozen chicken.

"I hate you, Andrew Pidgeon," I declared, raising it above my head. "And your stupid car!"

If that hateful outburst didn't make my feelings known,

my next move certainly did. I hurled the chicken as hard as I could, then took a step back and watched as it smashed through the windscreen of Andrew's beloved car.

Gill was the first to speak. "Bloody hell, Fiona," she muttered. "You've really done it this time."

Even in my cider haze, I knew I'd crossed the line. I also knew I'd gone too far to back down so I continued with the false bravado. "Hopefully it'll teach him a lesson," I replied, dusting my hands together.

"Well it taught me a lesson," said Charlene, still gripping her mystery meat for grim death. "Who knew chickens could fly?"

There wasn't time to enjoy the joke because Andrew disappeared from the window. We could still hear him though, screaming obscenities and calling me names as he made his way downstairs.

We listened to the furious tirade until the front door swung open, and then we did what any self-respecting young hoodlums would do.

We kicked off our shoes and legged it.

~

THE PLAYGROUND AT THE NURSERY SCHOOL ON GROVE ROAD was no place for three young women in the dead of night, but that's where we ended up.

I dropped my bag and shoes in the sand, and headed straight for the swing. "Someone give me a push," I called.

My two friends wandered over, both looking knackered and breathless. "You don't need a push," panted Gill. "You need an alibi."

Gill was the authority when it came to deviant acts. She'd been in enough scrapes of her own to know that trashing someone's car could end in a whole world of trouble, but I wasn't bothered in the least.

"He won't do anything about it." I kick-started the swing, slowly gaining height by swinging my legs. "Andrew's the one in the wrong, not me."

Charlene sat down on the end of the slide. "You poor thing," she said sadly. "You must be devastated."

When the swing glided forward I threw my head back, enjoying the cool breeze on my face. I felt far from devastated. The night was quiet, the stars were bright, and all I felt was free.

"I'm really not," I replied. "I feel wonderful."

Gill didn't seem to be listening. "We won't tell anyone what happened," she offered. "No one needs to know."

I dug my feet into the sand, bringing the swing to an abrupt halt. "Tell everyone. I don't care."

Finally giving up on her attempt at saving the mystery meat package from harm, Charlene unceremoniously dumped it in the sand. "I thought you loved him."

"I thought I did too," I replied. "But I know now that I don't."

"Because he's a cheater?"

"No," interjected Gill. "Because he's a dickhead."

Even after all that had happened, I couldn't bring myself to agree with her. He was spineless and weak, but I was too.

"We just want different things."

I wanted toe-curling passion and love and children. He wanted Mandy Brewer.

Charlene stood up and brushed herself off. "I think you're in denial, Fi," she said matter-of-factly. "Getting married was your dream, and it's just disappeared in a puff of smoke and chicken. You won't know what to do with yourself now."

It was a perfect time to confess that I'd been wanting to

call it off for days, but I didn't. I was too focused on Charlene's concern that my life was all but over.

"Do you really think I'm that one track?" I asked, slightly
miffed.

She shrugged but didn't speak, paving the way for Gill to
put her two cents in. "You don't talk about much else these
days, Fi."

The sprint to the playground must've sobered me up.
When I leapt off the swing, I managed to land on my feet.
"Maybe it's time to reinvent myself then."

"Well, you went ginger," Gill reminded me. "That didn't
work out so well."

Charlene dropped her head, directing her laugh at the
sand. My baleful glare only lasted until Gill cracked, and two
seconds later we were all in a fit of hysterics.

~

I WAS SURE THE WORST WAS OVER, BUT WHEN I ARRIVED HOME
to find Mam waiting for me at the foot of the stairs, I knew it
wasn't. Her expression was doleful, and in that instant, I
knew the bad news had beaten me home.

"Alright, Mam?" I asked.

"Mrs Roberts has been on the phone," she said flatly. "She
said my daughter was out raising hell on Darnley Road."

"Nosy old cow," I muttered under my breath.

Mam jumped to her feet quicker than I thought possible.
"You know the neighbours are vigilant," she snapped.

"Not always, Mam," I said bravely. "No one called to tell
you that Andrew was shagging Mandy Brewer."

Ordinarily, use of that kind of language would've come
with the threat of a slap, but my mother didn't say a word.
Instead, she began fussing with the curlers in her hair as if
she was passing time until I spoke again.

"Just so we're clear," I muttered, manoeuvring past her to get to the stairs. "The wedding is off."

"Don't be so hasty," she urged, grabbing my elbow. "Cooler heads will prevail in the morning. Just weather the storm."

Her archaic advice was maddening, but not unexpected. The older I got, the clearer it became that my father had deserted us of his own volition. God knows my mother wouldn't have kicked him out. She would've turned a blind eye and ignored his affair with the Gloucester Arms barmaid because in her mind, that's what a good wife does.

"Andrew ended it, Mam." I shrugged my arm free. "There is no storm to weather."

Too exasperated to continue the conversation, I stomped up the stairs. When I reached the landing, Mam called up to me. "Well, what are you going to do now, Fiona?"

My reply came at warp speed. "I'm going to stop wasting my time with idiots and find the boy who loves me."

DIARY OF FIONA BLACK

WEDNESDAY AUGUST 4, 1983

Tonight I lost my fiancé, and not even the sight of my wedding dress hanging on the back of my bedroom door makes me feel sad about it.

It's a pretty dress, but not the one I dreamed about. I don't want plastic pearls and cheap lace. I want dupioni silk and diamantes. Perhaps that's why I'm not sad.

Andrew Pidgeon is plastic pearls and cheap lace.

Book of the week: Sky High Lovers

Honeymoon Fund: £65.00

CHAPTER 12

THE NEXT FEW DAYS WERE TERRIBLE FOR MY MOTHER. IT WAS left to her to notify the guests that the wedding was off, and she did it with the cool disposition of a funeral director.

When one of my aunts dared to ask for details, Mam shot her down in flames. "The girl came to her senses," she snapped. "And that's all I'm going to say on the matter."

I flinched as she slammed the phone down, but Mam remained steadfast. "No one asked questions when her Ruby took off with that Tony fella from the key cutters," she said.

"That's because Toni was a girl, Mam," I reminded her. "Everyone was too confused to ask questions."

I'd always considered the reason behind my cousin's broken engagement fascinating, but my mother was far too old-school to talk about it.

"The whole world's gone bleedin' mad." She snatched her address book off the table and marched out of the room, leaving me chuckling to myself.

I hadn't seen or heard from Andrew since the chicken debacle. I once thought I heard his car passing along our street, but when I peeked out the window, I realised the high pitched engine noise was coming from Mr Kershaw's lawnmower.

Sooner or later, he was going to have to deal with me. I didn't expect an apology, and I certainly didn't want him back. But what I did want was the Duran Duran record I'd left at his house.

My mother was appalled. "For goodness sake, girl," she growled. "Have some dignity. If you start badgering him he's going to think you want him back."

"My dignity is perfectly intact, Mam," I insisted. "And I'll make it perfectly clear to Andrew that I want Simon Le Bon, not him."

~

Confidence was at an all-time high as I rapped on Andrew's door. I was wearing my best dress, my makeup was dead perfect, and after spending the night before locked in the bathroom with a box of L'Oréal, my hair was now a lovely shade of brown called Royal Suede.

The plan was simple; ask for my record, wish him well and get the hell out of there.

Unfortunately, it wasn't that easy. When his front door opened, my steely resolve went out the window. To make matters worse, time hadn't healed any of Andrew's wounds. He was just as hostile as the last time I saw him. "What do you want, Fi?" he grumbled.

"I just want to talk."

After a long moment of deliberation, he opened the door wide and ushered me inside. "Five minutes," he permitted. "I've got stuff to do."

"By stuff, you mean Mandy?"

We were not off to a good start. My big, rejected mouth was getting the better of me and I wasn't sure if I was going to be able to reign it in.

"There's no point even talking about this," he said dully. "I've made my choice."

"*Your* choice?" I kept my tone calm by biting the side of my cheek. "Why is it your choice?"

"Because you chose everything else," he snapped. "I never wanted any of this wedding malarkey, Fiona. It was a runaway train from the get-go."

I wanted to slap him with my Mel Lazar bag, but managed to hold off by taking a step back. "You proposed to me, you idiot," I reminded him. "Why would you do that?"

I thought back to exact second in time that he asked for my hand in marriage. He had no ring, but as he got down on one knee in front of the guests at my nineteenth birthday party, he promised to buy me one.

After hitting his dad up for a small loan, he presented me with a modest but pretty gold ring a few days later. I loved it, but I loved the sentiment behind it even more. He'd chosen me above all others, and that meant everything.

I held up my left hand and wiggled my fingers. The small diamond twinkled in the light just as it always did, but the meaning behind it was long gone.

"I didn't bring a present," Andrew muttered.

Utterly confused, I dropped my hand and looked up at him. "What do you mean?"

His hands settled in his pockets and his shoulders lifted. "It was your birthday and when I got to your party, I realised I didn't have a present," he explained. "So I proposed instead."

Andrew spoke casually as if the words didn't matter, but it was a confession that wrecked me. We'd known each other our whole lives, and had been together since we were fourteen, and all of a sudden that counted for nothing.

"How could you be so cruel?" I whimpered the question. "I loved you."

He turned away from me and let out a pissed off growl. "No you flippin' didn't. I was never good enough for you. You still think you're going to end up living in a castle with servants and butlers," he said roughly. "You're not bloody royalty, Fiona."

"I know that." Acknowledging my lack of pedigree didn't put an end to the conversation. He wasn't done venting yet.

"You're a control freak," he continued. "Everything has to be in line with your master plan or all hell breaks loose. I can't live like that."

"Am I that awful?" I wondered out loud.

"No." A flash of remorse ghosted across his face. "You're dead pretty, and we've had some laughs. You're just a pushy little cow, that's all."

It was a statement that could've done with some serious tweaking, but I let it go in favour of asking another question. "When were you going to call the wedding off?"

"What do you mean?"

"Well, if I hadn't caught you at Mandy's, I'd be none the wiser."

His confused expression gave way to one of shame. "I wasn't going to call it off."

My eyes widened. "So you were going to go through with it?"

Andrew shook his head, telling me no. "I wasn't going to show up," he confessed. "Mandy and me were going to take off to Blackpool instead."

I wasn't being hit with the truth, I was being battered. Not only had she stolen my fiancé, she'd stolen my honeymoon too. My whole chest ached as my heart splintered, but

Andrew was faring much better. Leaving me standing near the door, he slumped down on the sofa. "It's such a relief to get the truth out," he breathed. "Don't you feel better now?"

"Blackpool was our dream place," I muttered, leaving his dumb question unanswered.

"I know," he casually replied. "Mandy loves it there too."

His lack of concern for my feelings had nothing to do with laddish naivety. A truer picture was coming together before my very eyes.

"I have to go." I reached for the door handle. "I shouldn't have come here."

Andrew jumped up and rushed over, wedging himself between me and the door. "Not so fast."

For the briefest of moments, I was hoping for the bitter-sweet, heartfelt farewell that I'd read a million times over in my novels. On paper, they were cliché and overdone, but I would've killed to hear him say something romantic and maudlin to wrap things up.

I will never forget the love we shared.

Our stars just burn too brightly together.

You will forever remain in my heart.

Any of those sentiments would've been gratefully accepted, but Andrew's words weren't anywhere near as sweet.

"What about my car, Fi?" he asked. "It's going to cost a packet to get my windscreen replaced."

I spent a long moment carefully studying the face of the boy I nearly married. For the first time since I walked in, I could see hope in his blue eyes – but it had nothing to do with me, which was perfect.

It afforded me the common sense to realise that not only did this man not love me, he never had. Andrew Pidgeon loved his car, and he loved Mandy Brewer.

I was flying solo, but gaining height by the second.

I slipped my engagement ring off and handed it to him. "Sell this," I instructed, pushing him out of the way of the door.

"That won't cover it," he complained. "The ring is hardly worth anything."

I let out a hard laugh. "Exactly," I agreed. "It means nothing and it's worth nothing."

DIARY OF FIONA BLACK

SATURDAY AUGUST 7, 1983

*I didn't get my Duran Duran record back, but it wasn't a
wasted trip.*
I got myself back instead.
To celebrate, I stopped in at Woolworths and bought a new one.
The sound quality is much better than the one I left at Andrew's.
*Ever since Gill spilled cider on it, the needle skips over Planet
Earth.*
*I need a new adventure. Lucky for me, I've got £61 saved up to
make it happen.*
Book of the week: Sky High Lovers
Adventure Fund: £61.00

I DEALT WITH THE ENDING OF MORE THAN ONE RELATIONSHIP that week. Mrs Crichton-Percy phoned on Sunday night to tell me that my services were no longer needed.

"Don't take it personally," she began. "We have different standards when it comes to cleanliness. Even with instruction, yours are not up to par."

It was impossible not to take offense, mainly because she was lying. I wanted to remind her of the time I found dog poop in her walk-in closet but didn't. Instead, I asked if she wanted me to return the Lazar handbag she'd given me.

Her condescending cackle filtered through the phone. "No, dear, it's last season's," she replied. "Besides, it's probably as close as you'll get to haute couture."

If my mouth had planned a snarky comeback, my brain was too slow. Before I managed to utter a word, she hung up. Unsure of what my next move should be, I called Mam into the room and broke the news.

"The pompous cow mentioned nowt about standards when I was discounting velvet hangers for her." She spoke with absolute contempt, which was precisely the show of support that I needed. "Who does she think she is?"

Nina Crichton-Percy thought she was the queen of Bramhall, but after meeting Judith Wiltshire I knew differently. I suspect that might've had something to do with my dismissal. Keen to set the record straight, I quickly brought my mother up to speed.

"Judith is dead posh, Mam," I said, still awed. "And she's dripping with diamonds the size of ice blocks."

I followed up with a childish twirl that made my skirt flare and my mother chuckle. "Stay in your lane, my girl," she urged. "There's none of that nonsense in your future."

No one could burst my fairy-tale bubble quicker than my mother. It made me wonder what she thought my future held now that marriage and housecleaning in Bramhall were off the agenda. She gave little away but her face was etched with worry.

"I have plenty of ace things coming my way, Mam," I reassured her. "Just you wait and see."

DIARY OF FIONA BLACK

MONDAY AUGUST 9, 1983

Something amazing happened!
Judith found out that New-Money-Nina gave me the sack so she
called me at Mam's shop and offered me a job!!
Things are definitely on the up.
Book of the week: Sky High Lovers
Adventure Fund: £61.00

THE WILTSHIRE'S HOUSE WAS TWICE THE SIZE OF MRS Crichton-Percy's. As I walked up the long cobbled driveway, I counted nine windows at the front, and that didn't include the double bevelled glass doors.

Matching flower pots lined the front steps, and the basket of petunias hanging from the gabled porch was so flippin' manicured that it didn't look real.

Cleaning this house was going to be hard slog, but I felt nothing but excitement as I tapped the huge brass knocker against the door.

Finally, Judith answered. "Fiona, darling," she crowed. "Right on time."

I couldn't have killed my goofy smile if I tried. "I was so happy to hear from you," I babbled. "I'm excited to be here."

"You don't appear excited." She looked me up and down. "Frankly darling, you look downright dowdy and drab."

Instantly regretting my decision to wear jeans and a T-shirt, I self-consciously folded my arms. "I always wear this when I'm working."

Her disapproving frown quickly gave way to a demure

giggle. "Oh, dear girl," she snorted. "You've misread the situation. I don't need another cleaner, I have three already."

Not asking for a thorough job description was an embarrassing oversight that Judith was keen to rectify. With a wave of her hand, she ushered me inside and led me into her huge front room.

"Sit down, darling," she instructed.

I was nervous for a few reasons. First, it was the most opulent room I had ever set foot in. Everything looked sparkly, precious and expensive. Second, I had no idea of the etiquette involved when it comes to sitting on a pristine white sofa.

When she repeated the command, I parked my butt, crossed my legs at the ankles and hoped for the best.

Judith sat opposite me. "I've taken on an incredible amount of charity work in the past few months," she said, readjusting the small cushion behind her back. "I'm in need of assistance. I think you'd be perfect."

"It sounds dead important," I replied. "What would I have to do?"

"Well, first of all, I want you to lose the word 'dead' from your vocabulary," she chided. "Unless something is actually dead, refrain from saying it."

It was a demand that would've cut most girls to the quick, but I took no offense. "I will never say it again," I promised, hand on heart.

"Wonderful," she replied. "For the most part I just need someone to run a few errands and make phone calls. Do you think you can handle that?"

The real question was; could I handle her? Judith Wiltshire was the most intimidating, woman I had ever met. She spoke bluntly and honestly, ignoring any threat of hurt feelings along the way. Perhaps that's why I agreed to give it my best shot.

Her ruby smile was blinding. "You'll do well darling," she assured me. "I have every faith in you."

Working for Judith was going to be nothing like my time with Mrs Crichton-Percy. She was a far more interesting study, and the curiosity was mutual. Once the formalities were out of the way, conversation turned to my broken engagement.

I tried to gloss over the ugly parts, but Judith was a stickler for details.

Over tea and cake, I served up the whole sorry saga beginning with frozen poultry and ending with the return of my trinket ring.

"No one shed a tear, and no hearts got broken," I said.

"Oh, Fiona." Judith set her cup and saucer down on the coffee table. "It sounds like you both dodged a bullet."

I couldn't deny that she was right. As much as I wished Andrew was pining the loss, I'm sure he felt as relieved as I did.

"I'm just glad it's over." Trying to avoid her pitying stare, I took a tiny sip of tea. "Now we can both move on and make new plans."

In truth, I had nothing planned beyond Wednesday night bingo but the instant her housekeeper bustled into the room waving a cordless phone in the air, that changed.

"It's the lady from the Sunkiss Foundation, Mrs Wilt-shire," she announced. "Calling from London."

Judith extended the long aerial and put the dead modern phone to her ear. "Hello, Valeria," she crowed. "It's so lovely to hear from you."

Valeria might've been the poshest name I'd ever heard, but when I silently chanted it in my head I realised it sounded like a venereal disease. In a bid to stop myself laughing out loud, I focused more on the one-sided phone conversation and less on VD.

From what I could gather, Valeria worked for the same charity as Judith and New-Money-Nina. She was waiting to take delivery of the dresses they were donating, and judging by Judith's incessant apologies, she was running out of patience.

"I can have them to you as early as tomorrow afternoon, Valeria," she assured her. "My girl will hand deliver them." Judith stopped pacing and turned to me. "Fiona is very reliable," she said. "And she knows London like the back of her hand."

My first instinct was to jump up and slap her for telling such wicked lies. I'd never been to London in my whole life.

But before panic could take hold, I forced myself to calm down and consider the bigger picture. The single life wasn't likely to be packed with excitement. I needed something new and adventurous, and it didn't take a genius to know that a whirlwind jaunt to London might be it.

DIARY OF FIONA BLACK

THURSDAY AUGUST 12, 1983

I know I promised never to say it again, but I'm dead excited!!
I'm catching the early morning train to London.
Charlene said I'll be a new woman when I get back but Gill isn't as
positive. She said that if the rape and murder statistics are true, I
might not come back at all.
To be on the safe side, I changed my choice of shoes. My pink heels
are dead stylish, but I can run faster in my flat jellies.
I'm going to deliver Judith's dresses to the VD lady in Notting Hill
and then the day is mine.
Buckingham Palace, here I come!
<u>Book of the week:</u> Sky High Lovers
<u>Adventure Fund:</u> £61.00

I'VE SEEN *MURDER ON THE ORIENT EXPRESS* THREE TIMES. Perhaps that's why my views on train travel are so jaded.

In my mind, I was going to dress to the nines, board a lovely train and spend three hours looking and feeling as glamorous as Jaqueline Bisset.

Unfortunately, it wasn't to be. Looking glam is hard to do when you're dragging a suitcase full of cocktail dresses along a crowded train platform. Not one person offered to help and I soon realised that was because it was every man and woman for themselves.

It was hard to understand the reason behind the rush to board. The seats weren't luxurious leather like the Orient Express. They were stain riddled heavy brown upholstery that reminded me of the floor mats in Andrew's Cortina.

The white broderie anglaise dress I was wearing had never been more impractical, but I wasn't deterred. Nothing was going to put a dampener on this day, even the wad of gum that was stuck to the wheel of my suitcase.

I laid a hanky across the seat, parked my butt and steeled myself for the three-hour journey ahead.

EUSTON STATION WAS A MADHOUSE. *LONDON* WAS A madhouse. Everywhere I looked, people were rushing around as if they were late for an appointment. The only people who seemed to be travelling at a normal pace were the tourists, and they were flippin' everywhere.

Negotiating the Tube was one of the more complicated tasks I'd dealt with in my lifetime, but I somehow pulled it off. I arrived in Notting Hill just after ten and made my way to Valeria's house.

The narrow white frontage gave little away, but I knew the inside would be just as grand as Judith's. I would've killed for a peek inside, but I didn't make it past the front door.

I was greeted by a portly man in a suit who took the suitcase from my grasp, thanked me for coming and sent me on my way.

I was only miffed for a moment. The instant I stepped back onto the street and breathed in the warm London air, I realised my work was done. The rest of the day was mine, and I was determined to make the most of it.

~

OF ALL THE TOURIST ATTRACTIONS IN LONDON, BUCKINGHAM Palace was the one that rated highest on my list. The instructions given by the clerk at the information desk at Victoria Station were perfectly clear: exit onto Buckingham Palace Road, turn right and keep walking. It was impossible to get it wrong, but after a twenty-minute walk with no palace in sight, I realised I'd somehow ballsed it up.

Studying the small map for the umpteenth time, I tried to figure out where I'd gone wrong.

"Are you lost, *Mademoiselle?*"

The smooth foreign voice in my ear was so flippin' exotic that I thought I'd imagined it. And when I lifted my head and looked at him, I was sure of it.

No one real could look that good. The only thing more perfect than his dashing looks, dark hair and broad shoulders was his dress sense.

He wore a blue Pierre Cardin shirt, and I was ninety-nine percent sure it was the real deal.

"*Mademoiselle,*" he repeated. "Are you alright?"

Was he kidding me? Meeting a drop-dead gorgeous French man on the streets of London was a storyline straight out of one of my romance novels.

I was flippin' perfect!

Luckily, my actual reply was a little more subdued. "I'm fine, thank you."

"Are you looking for something?" he asked.

Buckingham Palace was the answer, but the words came out wrong. "A wonderful new adventure that I'll remember forever."

Most people would've turned on their heels and legged it, but the dreamy French guy didn't look too perturbed. If anything, he seemed amused.

He smiled, and it was as flawless as the rest of him. "How long do you have?"

The rest of my life, I didn't reply.

"I have to be back at Euston Station by four."

"It'll be a short adventure, *Mademoiselle,*" he replied, checking the time on his watch. "What do you have in mind?"

This was an all or nothing moment. I had nothing to gain by holding back and nothing to lose by being forward. At four o'clock, I'd board my train back to Manchester and the handsome French man would slip into the same vault of memories that I kept all my favourite stories.

"Do you know any really posh restaurants?" I asked hopefully.

I had sixty quid burning a hole in my pocket. A fancy lunch seemed like the perfect way to spend some of it.

He dropped his head, smiling down at the ground. "I might know a few."

"*Really* posh?" I quizzed. "I'm talking silver trays and crystal glasses. The whole kit and caboodle."

He straightened up and folded his arms. "Are you always this forthright and direct?"

I was, and I suddenly felt very foolish because of it. I was acting like a half-wit, and wasn't sure how to rein myself in.

"What's your name?" I quietly asked.

"Jean-Luc Décarie," he replied. "And you are?"

"A pushy little cow from Denton," I mumbled.

His deep laugh was wonderful. "What's your name, *Mademoiselle?*"

To prove I wasn't totally void of manners, I extended my hand. "Fiona Black."

I would never have predicted his next move. Jean-Luc kissed the back of my hand. "It's nice to meet you, Fiona," he said. "It would be my pleasure to take you to lunch."

He couldn't possibly have been telling the truth, but I wasn't about to argue the point. I was too busy trying to remember how to breathe, which was a wonderful turn of events. It meant that for the first time in my life, I was giddy.

~

GETTING INTO CARS WITH STRANGERS IS NEVER A GOOD IDEA, but when Jean-Luc flagged down a passing cab, I didn't hesitate to get in. Perhaps it was because he held the door open for me – a chivalrous gesture that I'd never experienced before.

"The Grand Chancellor restaurant please, driver," he instructed.

When we arrived just a few minutes later, he handed the cabbie a tenner and told him to keep the change. I'd never experienced that before either.

Just as we got to the door, I grabbed Jean-Luc's arm and pulled him aside. "Do you think I'm underdressed?" It seemed like a fair question. The woman who walked in ahead of us was wearing four inch heels and a lace blouse. "I don't want people to stare."

"People will stare, Fiona," he smoothly replied. "But it will be for the right reasons."

"Right, then." I sucked in my stomach and smoothed my hands over my hips. "Let's do this."

When Jean-Luc offered his arm, I gratefully accepted, hooking my arm through his as if I needed the support.

I frequented places like the Grand Chancellor Restaurant all the time while reading, but being there in real life was something else. I wasn't sure how to carry myself, but Jean-Luc didn't seem to share my nervousness.

As we approached the man standing behind the tall wooden podium near the door, he asked for a table for two. "Something quiet," he requested.

"Of course, sir." The man grabbed two menus. "Right this way."

My accidental date couldn't have been much older than me. Referring to him as 'sir' seemed awfully strange, but nothing about the last hour had been normal.

I paid little attention to where I was walking as we were shown to our table. I was too busy checking the place out. No detail was too small or insignificant. I'd likely never set foot in there again and I wanted to remember everything.

The dark wood panelling, emerald coloured drapes and low hanging chandeliers gave it an old world feel. Every immaculately set table had a lit candle in the centre, and the mood lighting made it impossible to tell whether it was day or night outside.

I got through the formality of having the waiter pull my chair out for me, and bluffed my way through the process of having a napkin laid across my lap. But when he handed me a wine list and started prattling off his list of recommendations, my bravado began to slip.

Lunch at the Grand Chancellor was shaping up to be an ordeal, and something in my expression alerted Jean-Luc to the fact that I wasn't handling it well.

"A bottle of Pinot Grigio, please," he announced, snapping the wine list shut.

The waiter dipped his head. "Very good, sir."

Jean-Luc barely acknowledged him as he backed away from the table. His warm brown eyes were fixed firmly on me. "Do you like wine, Fiona?"

"I don't know," I replied. "I'm more of a cider kind of girl."

"Perhaps I shouldn't have ordered for both of us." He smiled, but I detected no hint of condescension behind it. "Would you like me to order something different?"

"Not at all." My eyes drifted down to the open menu in front of me. "I'd like you to order my food for me too. I have no flippin' idea what any of this is."

I was used to chips and eggs. From what I could tell, chips weren't even on the menu.

Jean-Luc let out a quiet chuckle. "I can do that," he offered. "Tell me what you like."

Most of it was gobbledygook, but something caught my eye. I'd eaten cod a million times – never with a honey reduction or a courgette flower beignet – but I was prepared to give it a try. "The fish looks okay."

He closed his menu and placed it on the table. "I hope it's wonderful," he said.

I lifted my head, studying his handsome face for much too long. "You must think I'm very strange," I mused. "Why did you agree to this?"

A bright smile swept his face. "I find you beguiling," he said. "In a good way, of course."

Perhaps beguiling was French for strange, but I wasn't sure so I didn't pass comment. Instead, I hit him with more questions.

"What do you do, Jean-Luc?"

"I'm a struggling law student," he replied. "I'm in my second year at King's College."

Clearly the struggle wasn't financial. Even I knew that King's is a very exclusive school. Attending students drink Pinot Grigio and wear designer shirts.

"Are you failing?"

It was a bold question to ask, but there's a certain level of confidence that comes with knowing that you're never going to see someone again. There was no need to be coy and reserved, and based on Jean-Luc's ensuing reply, I could only assume that he felt the same way.

"Almost," he admitted. "My English leaves a lot to be desired, and my written essays are suffering because of it."

I huffed out a sharp laugh. "Your English is better than mine."

He shook his head. "Not when I write."

I could see his frustration, and felt the sudden need to offer some encouragement. "That doesn't mean you're thick, Jean-Luc," I assured him. "I know plenty of thickos so I'm qualified to judge."

He laughed, and his whole demeanour changed. "I'm not thick, I'm just French," he said. "That's the crux of the problem."

I didn't consider it to be a problem at all. He had a dead gorgeous accent that matched his dead gorgeous face.

"I was supposed to meet with a tutor today," he revealed, pinning me with a thoughtful stare. "But I was presented with a better offer."

I smiled down at the tablecloth. "Well, I was supposed to be meeting with the Queen today," I embellished. "She's probably wondering where I am."

~

WHEN THE WAITER RETURNED TO OUR TABLE, HE WAS ARMED with a bottle of wine and a fancy silver bucket filled with ice. He poured our glasses, took note of our food orders and slipped away as quietly as he'd arrived.

Jean-Luc charged his glass. "What shall we drink to?" he asked.

I barely needed time to think about it. "Short but memorable adventures," I announced, clinking my glass against his.

It should've been a prelude to wonderful conversation, but after taking a slow sip of wine, silence set in. I didn't take it to heart. We were complete strangers, and changing that would take much more time than we had.

"Do you like to read?" I asked extraneously. "Reading will improve your grammar no end. I read all the time – romance mostly." I was babbling now and couldn't seem to stop. "My grammar is ace."

I wasn't offended by his doubtful expression. My rough vocabulary gave no hint of the talent I possessed when it came to the written word. I'd been an A student all through school, but the prospect of furthering my education with college or university had never appealed.

"Perhaps you should tutor me," Jean-Luc suggested. "It could be the perfect arrangement."

I grinned. "And what would you do for me in return?"

In a move as smooth as he was, he rolled the stem of his

glass between his fingers. "I'm sure I'd find a way to make it up to you."

I sat up straight, smoothing the napkin on my lap with both hands. "Well, if you're stuck for ideas, I love diamonds and perfume and champagne."

His lovely smile was bright. "You like champagne? We can order champagne."

I was shaking my head before he finished his sentence. "I don't know nowt about champagne," I confessed. "It'd be wasted on me."

Jean-Luc brought his glass to his lips. "Some people deserve to experience the finer things in life, Fiona," he said. "Don't sell yourself short."

It was hard to believe that his syntax skills were lacking. The bloke looked young, but spoke like a middle-aged English professor.

"How old are you?" I quizzed.

"I just turned twenty-three."

"Do you live with your parents?"

He shook his head, telling me no. "My mother passed away when I was young but my father is around," he replied.

"I'm so sorry," I uttered, mentally kicking myself for asking the intrusive question.

He let me off the foot-in-mouth hook with a bright smile. "Don't be," he replied. "Over the years, I've had three stepmothers to bridge the gap."

His light tone led me to believe that it wasn't a sore subject, but the embarrassment I felt was a sharp reminder that prying is never a good idea. In a bid to stop any more accidental brain snaps, I took a long sip of wine.

Jean-Luc must've realised that I'd reined myself in, and that it was left to him to continue the conversation. He volunteered an extraordinary amount of information in a short space of time – and I soaked in every word as if he was a real life novel.

Even though he was struggling, he enjoyed the intense workload that came with studying for a law degree.

"I'm also on the rowing team," he revealed. "We're doing quite well this year."

"I can tell."

He frowned. "How?"

Yet again, my refined brain lost out to my blunt mouth. "You have lovely broad shoulders."

His skin flushed pink all the way down to his neck, but he artfully escaped the chagrin by changing the subject.

I kept my eyes locked on his, doing little to hide the fact that I was hanging on every word.

During the university semesters, Jean-Luc lived in Holburn, in a place called Lincoln Fields. From what I could tell, it was a very posh area, but his flat, and the two room-mates he lived with were not.

"They're odd fellows," he explained. "But beggars can't be choosers."

I set my glass down on the table. "I don't think you're a beggar," I noted. "Beggars don't wear Pierre Cardin."

He dropped his head and looked down at his shirt. "You might be right," he conceded with a smile. "But money can't buy you decent flatmates."

It can, however, buy you honey glazed cod.

I could hardly tear my eyes from my plate as the waiter set it down in front of me. The elaborate presentation made the humble fillet of fish look like a gallery exhibit.

"Is something wrong?" asked Jean-Luc.

Maybe I looked as confused as I felt. "I'm not sure," I mumbled. "It looks like they've battered the flower instead of the fish."

A low chuckle escaped him. *"Beignet de fleur de courgette,"* he announced. "Fried zucchini flowers."

I swallowed hard, trying to quash the giddiness that was threatening to overtake me. This man was storybook perfect, and I couldn't have conjured up a dreamier bloke if I'd written him myself.

"I bet you say that to all the girls," I teased.

He gifted me a crooked grin. "I don't believe I've ever said that to anyone."

I put my hand to my heart in an exaggerated show of excitement. "You mean, I'm your first?"

"Yes, my darling," he replied, hamming it up. "You are my first fried zucchini flower."

~

I speculated that the easy conversation could've continued indefinitely, but it was an impossible theory to test because time wasn't on our side.

When it was time to leave, Jean-Luc insisted on accompanying me to Euston station.

I spent the cab ride solemnly gazing out the window, catching a final view of London as I racked my brain for something to say. Jean-Luc didn't have much to say either.

"I wish you had let me pay for lunch," I said finally.

"Stay for dinner and I'll let you pay."

His demeanour didn't match the bold suggestion. His voice was weak and his frown was strong.

"Are you worried that I'll say yes or no?"

"I'm not an impulsive person, Fiona," he replied. "I'm usually far more controlled when it comes to making life altering decisions."

"Life altering? Wow, Jean- Luc." It was impossible not to

smile. "The dinner you're planning must really be something."

"It could be," he hinted. "The company alone would be phenomenal."

I had no experience when it came to accepting compliments. Flirty innuendo was new to me too – but at least I recognised it.

I held his gaze. "I'd miss the last train."

"You could stay with me," he shot back.

In a tell-tale sign that highlighted my inexperience, my cheeks flushed with heat. "That would definitely be a life altering decision," I mumbled.

Jean-Luc had no idea he was flirting with a career virgin, and that wasn't his fault. I'd purposefully steered most of the conversation, making sure that the focus stayed on him.

He was worldly, confident and posh. Ordinarily, a man like that wouldn't give me the time of day, and I wasn't going to embarrass myself by pretending otherwise.

Jean-Luc reached for my hand. "I'd like to get to know you better, Fiona."

His face fell as I gently broke his hold. "I think you'd be disappointed," I replied.

As if on cue, the taxi pulled into the parking bay outside the station. Dreading an awkward goodbye, I threw open the door and scrambled out. Jean-Luc tossed some money to the driver and quickly followed suit.

"Don't you think I should decide for myself?" He stepped in front of me, blocking my path. "I like to think I'm a good judge of character."

I couldn't deny that his persistent streak was good for morale. I'd never been pursued before (except by the cats that lurk near the fish and chip shop) but still, I couldn't give in.

A week ago, I had been engaged to be married, and it had

all ended in a hail of frozen poultry. There was just no way of explaining it without looking a fool.

I reached, lightly touching his arm. "I'll remember this day forever, Jean-Luc," I told him. "Good luck with law school."

To my own ears it sounded banal and inadequate, but he was even more unimpressed.

"I am French, Fiona." I could hear the smile in his voice. "Is that the best you've got?"

I must be crazy, I thought.

Jean-Luc Décarie ticked boxes that I didn't even know existed before now. In a few short minutes, he'd be gone forever – and my parting gesture was a pat on the arm.

Drawing on the only experience I had, I ripped off the plot of every romance novel I've ever read. I lurched forward, threw my arms around his neck and kissed him for all I was worth.

If it caught him by surprise, Jean-Luc didn't let on. He reciprocated, wrapping his arms tightly around me and holding me close.

Until then, I had no idea that a kiss could feel that flippin' tremendous.

Just like Angelica in *A Recipe for Romance*, a tidal wave of molten lava had burnt my heart to a cinder.

I was content to kiss him until I passed out, but Jean-Luc eventually called time. He took a step back, but his hold on me never wavered. "Are you sure you're not French, *Mademoiselle*?" he teased.

At that moment, I realised that I could be whoever I wanted to be. In my heart, I was royalty, and I'd finally met a boy who was treating me accordingly.

"Oh, sod it," I muttered, breaking free.

Jean-Luc looked as anxious as I felt, but he patiently waited while I rummaged around in my bag. My nerves were so shot that my hands shook, but I managed to find what I was looking for – my beloved diary.

I thumped it against his chest. "I want you to read this – every last word."

Ignoring my obnoxious tone, he asked what it was.

I couldn't blame him for being clueless. The tattered, dog-eared notebook gave no hint of the secrets it held.

"It's the last two years of my life," I nervously explained. "If you read it, you'll know everything about me. Good, bad and ugly, it's all there."

He smiled down at the book in his hands, slowly running his finger along the edge of the worn binding. "And if I like what I read?"

I dipped my head, chasing his brown eyes. "Come and find me," I told him. "I'll be waiting for you."

The End

PART II

SILK QUEEN

BOOK TWO

By G.J. Walker-Smith

CHAPTER 1

JEAN-LUC

WHEN I STARTED UNIVERSITY IN LONDON, I WANTED THE whole experience, and that meant stepping out of my comfort zone.

I'm not a gregarious, outgoing person. Sharing a place with a couple of random flatmates was supposed to change that, but after living with them for over a year I had to concede that I was no further along in my quest.

My choice of roommates probably had something to do with it. Describing them as odd would've been an understatement. Dmitry was a Russian exchange student, studying for a degree in molecular biology. By all accounts, he was a brilliant man – he just didn't act like it. He rarely left his room, and when he did, it was only to check if the phone was bugged. I once asked why, and immediately wished I hadn't.

"Eventually, they will find us," he gravely warned. "Be ready."

To this day, I don't know who 'they' are, but if they ever do show up, I pray that they kidnap him and return him to his home planet.

My other roommate was just as eccentric, but marginally

easier to deal with. By day, Gordon was a thirty-something mild-mannered accountant. By night, he was Rhiannon, the leading cabaret act at the Fizzy Oyster nightclub.

Gordon wore grey suits and wide plaid ties. Rhiannon favoured corsets and fishnet stockings, which was perfectly fine unless they were left airing in the bathroom.

It wasn't an ideal living arrangement, but I was slowly getting used to it. I like structure and rules, and to stop ourselves from killing each other, we'd implemented many. Most of the time, things ran smoothly, and when they didn't we'd call a meeting and sort it out.

Historically, the act of calling a house meeting was reserved only for emergencies – like our inability to deal with the horror of finding Rhiannon's false eyelashes stuck to the soap – but my reason for calling that day's meeting was no one's emergency but my own.

It had been nearly a week since my impromptu lunch date with enchanting Fiona Black. I read her diary from cover to cover more times than I was willing to admit, but to say I understood her better would be a lie. From what I could tell, she was incredibly smart but not the least bit studious. Fiona was naïve to the point of silliness, and yet wise beyond her years. She didn't suffer fools, but had come dangerously close to marrying one, and she had a penchant for using the word 'dead' when describing something good.

I was confounded, and unusually intrigued, which meant the only option I had was to follow through with her wild suggestion of heading to Manchester to find her.

As far as spontaneity goes, that's where it ended. The rest of the plan would require serious organisation and an awkward conversation with my flatmates.

Dmitry arrived right on time. He slipped out of his bedroom, quickly checked the phone for bugs and then sat down at the table.

I knew better than to question why he was wearing a sheet of tin foil on his head, and I tried my best not to stare. With a stiff nod, I thanked him for coming.

The flat's only communal living space was the small dining room next to the kitchen. A more casual setting might've made house meetings more tolerable, but as things stood, I was stuck sitting opposite a Russian madman.

"I have travelled very far to be here," Dmitry claimed in a monotone voice.

I could see his bedroom door from where I sat. I didn't question that either. "I appreciate the effort," I said.

After a long wait, Rhiannon finally burst through the door. I would have much preferred to deal with Gordon, but as she explained, it was rehearsal day at the Fizzy Oyster.

"Rehearsal ran late," she said, dumping her huge bag on the table. "But I'm here now. What's this all about?"

"I've met someone," I announced, getting straight to the point. "And I'd like to invite her to stay here for a while."

Dmitry leaned closer to me, making his foil hat crackle. "To monitor us?" he asked.

"No," I replied. "To spend time with me."

"When?" asked Rhiannon.

"I don't know."

She shrugged. "Well, how long will she be staying?"

"I don't know."

"You're very light on details, Jean-Luc," she replied. "It seems dodgy to me."

Quite the opposite was true. I had plenty of details about the girl in question, but I wasn't willing to share them. All I needed from them was permission to have her visit.

Dmitry turned to Rhiannon. "She is mail order bride," he said knowingly. "Very common in Russia."

Rhiannon stared me down from across the table, slowly

shaking her head. "He wouldn't order a wife," she speculated. "A prostitute, maybe."

Unsure who to direct my outrage toward, my eyes darted between both of them. "She's just a friend," I snapped. "And I didn't pay a cent for her."

"Settle down, Napoleon," said Rhiannon. "There's no need to get all French about it. We're just curious."

As much as it pained me, I needed them on side so I didn't bite back. Instead, I pulled in a calming breath and gave them a very short run down of our chance meeting and impromptu lunch date.

Rhiannon seemed far more interested than Dmitry.

"Love at first sight?" she asked.

I shook my head. "There is no such thing."

Her thick green eye makeup creased as she smiled. "It's a very real phenomenon, Jean-Luc," she insisted. "Sweaty palms, rapid heartbeat and a skip in your step. Those are the signs."

Dmitry pulled a tissue from his pocket and covered his nose and mouth. "It could also be a virus," he said jumping to his feet. "You should be quarantined."

Before he bolted to his bedroom, I asked an important question. "Do I have your blessing to bring Fiona here, Dmitry?"

"Yes." He flapped his hand at me. "But make sure she's clean."

His door slammed shut and Rhiannon rose to her feet. "You have my blessing too," she said, slinging the end of her feather boa over her shoulder. "And for your sake, I hope she's a little bit dirty. All work and no play makes Napoleon a very dull boy."

CHAPTER 2

JEAN-LUC

PERHAPS I WAS LOSING MY MIND. GIVEN THE CURRENT STATE of my grades, missing classes in favour of a mid-week jaunt up north was reckless and irresponsible, but I barely hesitated. Armed with nothing more than a tattered diary and a dose of bravado, I boarded a train to Manchester and headed into the proverbial unknown.

Playing detective wasn't my strongpoint but after a quick search of the Yellow Pages I managed to track down the address of the haberdashery shop owned by Fiona's mother.

I picked up a cab and headed straight over there but as I stood on the pavement looking up at the sign above the door, urgency began to slip. I had no idea if Fiona would be there, or what I would say to her if she was, but with no option but to forge ahead, I took a deep breath and went inside.

The second the bell at the top of the door jingled, a gruff woman snapped at me. "We're closing. It's six o'clock."

"I'm not here to purchase anything, Madame," I replied.

"No hawkers." She picked up a broom thrust it forward as if she was trying to sweep me out of the door. "On yer way."

"I'm looking for Fiona Black," I quickly explained. "Is she here?"

The woman relaxed her grip on the broom. "Fiona is my daughter."

It was a revelation that brought me comfort and terror in equal measure. I'd successfully tracked Fiona down, but on the downside, her mother was a broom-wielding tyrant.

"Is she here?" I asked hopefully.

"No."

My hands settled in my pockets. "Well, do you know where I might find her?"

"Yes."

I was getting nowhere incredibly fast. I tried to soften her by introducing myself but she cut me off in an instant.

"I know who you are," she grumbled. "You're the French boy she met in London." She leaned her weapon against the wall and stood behind the counter. "What are you doing here?" she asked. "Is Fiona expecting you?"

I wanted to say yes but I had to admit that I'd arrived on a whim. "I'd like to invite her to come to London for a while, with your permission of course."

She huffed out a sharp laugh as if the notion was absurd. "My daughter is twenty-years-old," she reminded me. "What kind of mother would let her run off with a strange man she knows nothing about?"

"I'm not strange," I declared, hand on heart. "I have the utmost respect for your daughter."

I knew it was an impossible sell. Reading Fiona's diary had given me valuable insight regarding her family dynamics. Mrs Black kept tight reins on her daughter, and she wasn't likely to loosen her grip any time soon.

The crotchety woman grabbed a bolt of fabric off the counter and placed it on a nearby shelf. "Fiona hasn't stopped talking about you in days," she revealed. "She thinks you're some sort of wealthy prince charming."

I wanted to smile but thought better of it. "I have no royal connections."

Her eyes narrowed. "Did you lie about being wealthy too?"

I frowned. "I haven't lied about anything."

Mrs Black turned around and hoisted a large roll of blue fabric off the shelf. "This is dupioni silk." It hit the counter with a thud. "My daughter is convinced that all of her dresses will be made of this one day."

"Is that a problem?" I asked, confused.

"It's ten quid a yard," she replied staring straight at me. "So it's not likely to happen."

I shrugged, unwilling to speak until I knew where she was heading.

"I couldn't care less whether you're rich or poor, lad," she told me. "But if you've promised my girl silk and follow through with cotton, I'll bury you."

For a hundred different reasons, Mrs Black was terrifying, but I battled on like a trooper. I pointed at the roll of silk. "How much is that?"

"I told you," she replied. "Ten quid a yard."

"For the whole lot," I clarified, reaching for my wallet.

The corner of her mouth lifted as she checked the tag. "There's forty-eight yards here," she replied. "Five hundred quid."

"No, that equals four hundred and eighty pounds."

"Are you cotton or silk, lad?" she baited.

I was silk, and the wad of crisp notes that I slapped down on the counter proved it. "So you'll let Fiona accompany me back to London?"

Mrs Black snatched the money off the counter and

counted it. "No," she snorted. "You bought silk, not my daughter."

"I'm not trying to buy her." It was impossible to keep the frustration from spilling over, but I tried. "I'm merely trying to – "

"Go to the bingo hall on Yardley Road," she cut in. "That's where you'll find her tonight."

CHAPTER 3

JEAN-LUC

I QUICKLY CONCLUDED THAT BINGO IS NOT FOR THE FAINT OF heart. There must've been at least a hundred people inside the hall, but no one paid me a skerrick of attention as I slipped through the front doors. Every one of them had their eyes glued to the cards on the table in front of them, marker pens at the ready.

A man stood on the stage at the front, cranking the handle on a big round cage of coloured balls. As one fell through the chute, he scooped it up and handed it to the woman standing next to him.

She brought her microphone to her mouth. "Rise and shine, twenty-nine," she boomed, waving the ball in the air.

It wasn't a popular number. The mass mumbling that broke out was unintelligible, but most definitely hostile. When a very excited lady jumped out of her seat and yelled 'bingo' a few moments later, I actually feared for her safety.

No one was muttering now. The hall was filled with a loud array of angry growls and unsportsmanlike groans.

The lady with the microphone put a swift end to the

discontent by announcing a half hour break. "Make sure you're back here by quarter past," she instructed.

Clearly, the doorway was not the best place to be as the mass exodus took place. I was pushed outside, somehow managing to end up curb-side with the smokers. I was never going to find Fiona at this rate, and the defeat was beginning to show.

"What's to do with yer, lad?" The lady beside me took a long drag of her cigarette. "You look lost."

"I'm looking for someone," I replied, waving my hand to clear the smoke. "Do you know – "

"Me, me, me!" yelled a voice from behind. "He's looking for me!"

Fiona determinedly pushed her way through the crowd, making the old woman chuckle. "Easy lass," she called. "Don't want to appear too eager, do yer?"

As far as I was concerned, there was no such thing as appearing too eager. I'd been second guessing myself all day, but every trace of doubt disappeared the second Fiona threw her arms around me – and the chokehold she held on my neck led me to think she was in a good place too.

Taking her cue to leave, the smoking lady stubbed out her cigarette and bade us goodnight. As soon as she was out of earshot, I whispered in Fiona's ear, "Good evening, *Mademoiselle.*"

She inched her head back to look at me. "I can't believe you came."

"I had to," I replied, lowering her to her feet. "I liked what I read."

Her bright smile took the edge off the cool night air. "What happens now?" she asked.

I managed to smile and frown at the same time. "Don't you have a plan?"

"Of course I do," she beamed. "I just want to make sure it's the same as yours."

"I want you to come back to London with me." It was a simple plan, but apprehension kept my voice small. I had no idea how I'd save face if she said no. "I thought we could spend some time getting to know each other."

"You've read my diary, Jean-Luc," she reminded me. "You know everything."

"Perhaps," I agreed. "But I don't keep a diary so you'll have to get to know me the old-fashioned way."

"I want to know everything about you," she said, reaching for my hand. "And I hope it takes a really long time."

It was a hopeful comment that was absent of all innuendo. Fiona was nothing like the spoiled, boorish socialites I usually dealt with, and that was part of her charm.

I gave her hand a gentle squeeze. "I'm glad I came here."

"Me too," she replied. "Where are you staying tonight?"

Her question made me cringe. I'd organised my trip to Manchester the same way I organised all my trips – by enlisting the services of a travel agent. But as I stood outside the local bingo hall in downtown Denton, I realised what an obnoxious move it was. And I now had to confess that I was booked into the Palladium Hotel.

"Are you flippin' kidding me?" she asked, eyes wide. "Gill went to a wedding reception there once. She said it's like a palace inside."

"I'd love to take you there," I replied. "But I promised your mother that you'd be home early."

Fiona dropped my hand. "You spoke to my mam?"

"I went to her shop," I explained. "I didn't know where else to find you."

"Did she give you a hard time?" Her voice was filled with worry. "She wasn't keen on the idea of you coming here."

"I think I won her over."

And I had forty-eight yards of silk in my hotel room to prove it.

"She might not let me go, Jean-Luc," she replied, speaking down at the pavement. "She thinks pinning my hopes on a boy I hardly know is ugly behaviour."

I dipped my head, chasing her eyes. "What did you tell her, exactly?"

"The truth," she mumbled. "I met a boy in London, and I have a feeling that he's going to change everything."

I'd been privileged my whole life, but never more than at that moment. If this adventure went no further than a week in London, I'd be forever grateful to this girl. She'd forced me out of my comfort zone and dared me to take a chance.

"You've already changed me," I confessed. "I've never done anything this crazy before."

"Me neither." Her lovely smile was bright. "But I'm game if you are."

A very vague plan was hatched over the next few minutes. Fiona gave me her address and asked me to pick her up there in the morning.

"I'll break the news to Mam tonight," she said. "And with a bit of luck, she won't break me."

I wanted to remind her that she was an adult who was free to make her own decisions, but I had no experience when it came to dealing with strict parents so it wasn't my place to comment.

Fiona grabbed my wrist and checked the time on my watch. "Interval is nearly over," she said. "Will you come inside and meet my friends?"

"Of course," I replied. "I would love to."

That was a lie. I'd read about her friends in great detail. One was a ditzy brunette with an extensive stuffed toy collection and the other was a hot-headed blonde with an extensive juvenile record.

Despite this knowledge, I followed Fiona inside. The hall was mostly empty but a few diehard players were still seated, readying themselves for the next round of play by lining up their marker pens.

"Bingo is a very serious game, isn't it?" I whispered from the corner of my mouth.

Fiona let out a soft giggle. "There's not much else to do around these parts."

Not everyone took such a hard-core approach. As we closed in on a table near the stage, a petite brunette jumped out of her seat and let out a squeal that echoed through the hall. "Is this the French bloke?" she asked, rushing at us.

Fiona stepped closer to my side. "Yes, Charl," she confirmed. "This is Jean-Luc."

The gesture of extending my hand was wasted on Charlene. Instead of meeting my handshake, she spun back to face the surly blonde who had remained at the table. "I told you he was real, Gill," she snapped.

She shrugged. "Never said he wasn't."

Fiona's cheeks flushed a pretty shade of pink. "Ignore them," she muttered.

Charlene grabbed me by the elbow and pulled me toward the table. "Sit with us," she urged. "They're going to start calling numbers again soon."

"Oh, I'm not playing," I told her. "I wouldn't know how."

"It's not rocket science," interjected Gill, pushing out the chair beside her. "I'm sure a hotshot like you could get the hang of it."

I sat down because I didn't feel like I had a choice in the matter. If I refused, Gill was likely to subdue me with a headlock.

"You can use my lucky green pen," said Charlene, thrusting it at me. "It matches your eyes."

Gill leaned, quickly studying my face. "His eyes are brown, yer dozy mare."

"I said it *matches* his eyes, Gill," she snapped. "I didn't say it was the same colour."

I found the banter amusing, but Fiona sat down next to Charlene and quickly put a stop to it. "We're not playing the last half." She snatched the pen from my hand. "I have to go home and pack. I just came in to say goodbye."

Gill's eyes widened to the size of saucers. "You're going to London?"

"Sure am." Fiona glanced at me and smiled. "I'm going to hang out with Jean-Luc for a while."

Charlene slumped back in her chair and let out a wistful sigh. "So flippin' romantic, Fi," she said. "We send you outside to get a bag of crisps and you come back with a fairy-tale."

Fiona's diary was filled with musings of hope for the future. It made sense that her best friends were privy to her plans, but it added an element of pressure that made me uncomfortable.

Mercifully, Fiona quickly set the record straight. "Jean-Luc is not a fairy-tale. He's not a ticket out or some sort of saviour either." She darted her eyes between her two friends. "I don't need saving."

Gill leaned past me, looking toward the door. "We're all going to need saving in a minute," she grumbled. "Mandy and Sharon just walked in."

I didn't need to ask a single question. I was well-versed when it came to the antics of Mandy Brewer and her friend Sharon, and I was clued up enough to know that an ugly confrontation was probably forthcoming.

Mandy was a slight girl, but clearly a big character. She sauntered down the aisle between the tables, carrying herself as if she was important. I knew a thousand girls just like her – but none who wore plastic pearls and crop tops. Sharon's style was far less showy, which was probably a good thing. The woman was brutish, and she walked like a lorry driver.

"Just ignore them, Fi," urged Charlene.

"Bollocks to that," snapped Gill. "Introduce them to your new man." She motioned to me with a nod. "Tell them you've met a rich new bloke who's whisking you off to the French Riviera."

It was a ridiculous embellishment, but I would've gone along with it if she'd asked me to.

"I'm not going to lie," Fiona whispered. "I've got no reason to lie."

"She stole your fiancé," Gill reminded her. "You should tear her apart."

Fiona didn't reply, and seconds later, the woman who'd wronged her in the worst way imaginable was sidling up to the table.

"Move along," menaced Gill. "Your cheap perfume is stinking up the joint."

"It's not cheap," snapped Mandy. "It's Pure Silk."

"It's pure something alright," said Charlene.

Bulletproof and unaffected, Mandy set her sights on Fiona. "How are you, Fi?" Her sympathetic tone was nauseating. "Holding up okay?"

"I'm fine," she replied, straightening up in her chair. "Why wouldn't I be?"

Mandy smirked. "Being jilted at the altar must've been really humiliating for you."

"Going through with it would've been worse," she shot back.

The dynamics were impossible to understand. If anyone should've been embarrassed it was man-stealing Mandy but for some reason, she was claiming the upper hand.

"She doesn't need Andrew," defended Charlene. "She's moved on."

Figuring that was my cue, I slid my chair back and stood. "Jean-Luc Décarie," I said, holding out my hand.

Mandy looked at my hand but didn't move. "Who are you?"

Perhaps her brain had seized and she missed my introduction. The vapid look on her face made the notion seem entirely possible.

Gill jumped in. "He's what happens when you stop laying down with dogs," she said.

Mandy extended her hand as if she was the first to make the gesture. "I guess one man's trash is another man's treasure."

I didn't shake her hand. Instead, I turned my sights on Sharon, who was sniggering beside her. "You must be Darren," I baited.

After a few seconds of stunned silence, a fit of muffled giggles broke out across the table. Mandy ordered them to shut up, but her friend's murderous glare was reserved entirely for me.

"It's Sharon," she corrected through gritted teeth.

"My mistake." I put my hand to my heart and dipped my head. "I called it as I saw it."

"You're rude," hissed Mandy.

"And you're a terrible waste of my time," I retorted.

"Mine too." Fiona rose to her feet. "Ready to go, Jean-Luc?"

I'd never been readier, but replied with a casual nod.

"Where are you going?" asked Mandy.

Finally, Fiona smiled. "To London."

"To visit the queen?" The posh accent Mandy adopted didn't convey an ounce of class.

"No, I'm not going to visit the queen." Her voice was low and serious. "I'm going to London to be one."

CHAPTER 4

JEAN-LUC

THE PROMISE I'D MADE TO MRS BLACK OF HAVING HER daughter home at a respectable hour was one I couldn't keep. Fiona decided that she wasn't going to give up the chance to check out the inside of the Palladium Hotel and I had no desire to talk her out of it.

As soon as the cab pulled up under the canopied entrance of the hotel, she scrambled out before the doorman had a chance to open the door.

"Cheers," she greeted, smiling brightly.

The bemused man tipped his hat. "Good evening, Madam."

Fiona spun back to face me. "This is dead posh, Jean-Luc," she said. "He's wearing flippin' gloves, and all."

I had no idea how to reply, so I didn't. Instead, I slipped the doorman some money, grabbed Fiona's hand and led her through the doors of the Palladium Hotel.

AS FAR AS HOTEL SUITES GO, I WOULD'VE RATED MINE FOUR

stars. Fiona walked through the door and instantly rated it an impossible nine-and-a-half.

"Is that all?" I teased. "Why not ten?"

She darted her eyes around the room. "I was expecting fruit baskets and chocolates," she replied. "I'm famished."

I chuckled my way over to the desk and picked up the room service menu. "Order whatever you like," I said, handing it to her.

Fiona sat down on the edge of the bed and placed the menu on her lap. "Are you laughing at me?"

"Of course not," I replied.

"I have no clue what I'm doing here, Jean-Luc," she said in dismay. "London will be worse so taking me back with you is madness. I don't know how to act or what to say. You'll think I'm an idiot."

I appreciated the show of vulnerability no end. After feeling out of my depth all day, it somehow put us on a more even par.

"I would never think that, Fiona." I laid my jacket across the nearest chair and sat down beside her. "I think you're beguiling, remember?"

"Still in a good way?" she asked, nudging me with her shoulder.

"In the best way."

"But can you spell it?" she asked, finally breaking a smile. "If you're going to use a fancy word like that you should at least know how to spell it."

I looked to the floor, trying to stop the burning in my cheeks from taking hold. "Probably not with any accuracy."

Fiona stood up and grabbed a pen off the desk. "Fancy," she said, examining it closely. "I bet these get nicked all the time."

She sat beside me and reached for my hand. I didn't say a

word as she slowly scratched the black pen across my open palm. I didn't look at it either. My focus was reserved entirely for her, and it had been that way since the minute we'd met.

"There," she announced, clicking the pen. "B-e-g-u-i-l-i-n-g."

I held up my hand, studying the word carefully. "I shall never forget it," I promised, taking the pen from her grasp. "But I think the education should be mutual."

I caught a faint smell of her flowery perfume as she craned her neck, which made concentrating difficult. But with a careful touch of the sharp pen, I wrote a word that I wanted her to remember forever. "*Enivrante*," I announced, releasing her hand.

Fiona studied her palm closely. "What does it mean?"

A less invested version of myself might've tried charming her with a cliché French word that had been used a million times over, but it would've counted for nothing. I'd chosen something far more important instead.

"Completely and utterly smitten," I explained, tossing the pen back on the desk.

Her worried expression slipped in an instant. "My friends think you're too good to be true," she revealed. "I really hope they're wrong, Jean-Luc."

"I have my faults," I confessed.

She leaned closer, boring into me with dark blue eyes. "But are you good?"

I honestly wasn't sure, and I told her so – even at the risk of having her walk out the door. "I have a very definite idea of the man I want to be," I said. "And in ten years from now, I'm going to be him."

It must've sounded ludicrous, but Fiona was far from perturbed by the prospect. She shuffled across the bed, fluffed up the stack of decorative pillows and settled back. "I guess I'll wait then." She smiled at me. "He sounds like an interesting bloke."

~

Spending the night together was purely accidental. It started out with an exorbitant amount of room service and ended when we both fell asleep after hours of talking. It was perfect – until the cold light of day forced us to re-join the rest of the world.

Fiona was a bundle of nerves, worried by the prospect of dealing with her mother. She was fidgety and distracted, but still determined to follow through with her trip so we picked up a cab outside the hotel and prepared to head into battle.

"Do you think you'll be in trouble?" I asked.

I deserved the harsh frown she gave. It wasn't a well thought out question. "I stayed out all night with a boy I hardly know, Jean-Luc. She's probably going to slaughter me."

I hoped she didn't mean literally, but there was no time to ask for clarification. The cab pulled up outside a row of modest terraced houses with identical white front doors. I picked the Black's address instantly, mainly because the furious lady of the manor came storming out to meet us.

"Ready?" Fiona asked.

It was too bad if I wasn't. Nellie was already thumping on the window.

I had no idea how long the slaughtering would take, but ever the optimist, I dropped a ten pound note over the driver's shoulder and asked him to wait.

"No promises," he replied. "I don't want no trouble."

Fiona was already out of the cab, pleading with her mother to keep her voice down.

138

"I'll do no such thing!" she roared. "I've been mithered to bleedin' death all night because of you."

"I'm sorry," replied Fiona. "I should've called."

Her apology fell on deaf ears as Mrs Black turned her wrath on me. "You've got some nerve, boy," she hissed.

Any headway I'd made when it came to winning her over was now null and void. I was back to square one, and clueless when it came to making amends.

Parental concern was an alien concept to me, but I respected it. In the calmest voice I could muster, I apologised to her. "I take full responsibility," I said. "Time just ran away from us."

Mrs Black pointed as if she was hexing me. "You keep your grubby mitts off my daughter."

Fiona moved, bravely standing between us. "He's not grubby, Mam," she insisted. "And his mitts were nowhere near me."

She was telling the absolute truth. The combination of bedroom hair and a night-before dress made for a sordid scenario, but the real version of events was much tamer.

"Nothing happened, Mrs Black."

She didn't look convinced, but she didn't rip my head off either. Instead, she put a firm hand on Fiona's shoulder and ordered both of us into the house.

Nellie's demeanour inexplicably changed once she got us behind closed doors. She dropped the choler from her tone and calmly invited me to sit down.

I didn't trust the change one bit, and Fiona didn't seem to be buying it either. "The cab is waiting, Mam," she reminded her.

And I'm sure he'll testify in court, I didn't add.

"Go upstairs and pack your things, Fiona." Nellie's eyes never left mine. "And don't forget your coat."

I was confused and unnerved, but determined to hold my

ground. As soon as Fiona was out of earshot, Nellie ramped up the menacing act. "Sit down," she demanded. "You and I are going to talk."

I took a few steps into the small front room and sat down on the settee.

"We call this the good room," she said, fluffing up a cushion on the armchair. "Reserved only for company and special occasions."

My eyes darted in every direction, silently taking stock of my surroundings. The dark green settee matched the brown shag carpeting and cream embossed wallpaper, and that's all there was to it. It was homely, pin neat and modest – but none of those words seemed complimentary enough so I stayed quiet.

"It's not quite what you're used to, is it?" she asked.

Reading between the lines has never been my forte, but I got where she was going in an instant.

"I don't judge people based on their circumstances," I replied. "And I hope I'm not judged because of mine."

She smirked as if I'd said something foolish, and perhaps I had. As far as social standing goes, we were poles apart and she knew it.

"Convincing Fiona that she's stumbled upon her fairy-tale ending won't be difficult, Jean-Luc," she told me. "But all the money in the world will count for nothing if you're a dirty scoundrel in prince's clothing."

"I'm not," I assured her.

Nellie settled back in the chair. "That remains to be seen, doesn't it?"

"With all due respect, Mrs Black, I have nothing to prove to you."

She shot me a baleful glare. "You have everything to prove to me," she snapped. "I'm not going to willingly throw my daughter to the first wolf who comes along."

Technically, I was the second wolf. She'd had no qualms when it came to throwing her in Andrew's direction – even after he'd proven himself to be the biggest dirty scoundrel of all. The hypocrisy was maddening.

"I know about Fiona's previous engagement," I revealed. "Perhaps you should've taken this hard line when vetting him."

My comment was rude and out of order. I expected her to collar me and throw me out the door, but she didn't.

"I've learned from my mistakes." Her tone was calm but her expression was fierce. "There won't be a repeat of that debacle."

"I haven't promised Fiona a fairy-tale ending, Mrs Black." It felt like an important point to make. "I haven't promised her anything."

"Keep it that way," she demanded. "The last thing she needs is to get carried away by fanciful notions that head nowhere."

It was a miracle that Fiona had remained so upbeat and hopeful in the face of such pessimism. Nellie Black's take on the world was nothing short of depressing.

"If that's how you feel, why are you letting her go to London?"

Her eyes darted around the room. "Because I want her to know more than this," she replied with a touch of melancholy. "And I can't give that to her."

CHAPTER 5

JEAN-LUC

RELEASING HER DAUGHTER TO THE WILD WASN'T unconditional. There were rules, and Nellie laid out all seven hundred of them in the time it took us to walk from the front door to the waiting cab.

"Don't take drugs," she warned. "And watch out for pick-pockets. I hear they're rife in London."

"I won't take drugs," Fiona assured her. "And my pockets aren't worth picking."

Nellie grabbed her by the elbow and pulled her to a stop. "Be sensible, my girl." Her voice was quiet and serious. "Make good choices."

"Oh, Mam." Fiona lurched forward and hugged her mother tightly. "I'll be home before you know it."

Nellie looked past her and shot me a nervous look. Better than anyone, Nellie knew that Fiona would likely hit the ground running, and as much as she wanted to believe that I was stealing her away, it had nothing to do with me.

~

When I made the decision to invite Fiona to London, I didn't consider how complicated the process would be. I wasn't used to complications. Unlike Fiona, I was raised to do whatever I pleased without restrictions.

My father didn't give a damn about the choices I made so it was up to me to make sure that the line I walked was straight and narrow. Nellie's approach with Fiona was much more hands on, and as I caught sight of her crestfallen expression as the cab pulled away, I was reminded that that was how it was supposed to be.

Perhaps I looked troubled by the notion. Fiona reached across and gave my hand a squeeze. "Are you alright?"

I glanced at her and smiled. "Absolutely fine."

"Would it be okay if we made one more stop?"

"Of course," I replied. "Anywhere you want to go."

Fiona shuffled forward and spoke to the driver, giving him directions to an address in Bramhall.

"My boss' house," she explained, turning back to me. "Judith has been so good to me. I'd like to tell her that I'm leaving in person."

It was a responsible, honourable thing to do but she quickly began second-guessing herself. "Maybe I shouldn't just turn up unannounced," she mused. "It's not really the done thing, is it?"

"I'm sure she'll appreciate the gesture," I said, trying to put her at ease.

In her diary, Fiona had described Judith Wiltshire as being the classiest woman in existence. With an endorsement like that, I expected to meet a genteel woman of polite society but the woman who answered the door fell short of my expectations.

The lady epitomised new money – crisp white pantsuit, far too much jewellery and a fluffy white dog in her arms.

"Fiona, darling," she crowed, completely ignoring me. "I wasn't expecting you today."

Fiona apologised, which was a ludicrous act brought on by nerves. "I just wanted to let you know –"

Judith rudely cut her off by loudly beckoning her house-keeper. As soon as the young woman appeared by her side, she offloaded the dog into her arms. "Take Monty," she demanded. "And bring some tea for our guests."

With a wave of her hand, she ushered us through to the living room and continued barking orders from the foyer. "Some cake too, Nola… but not those wretched lemon bars. They were ghastly."

I sat down beside Fiona. She smoothed out her skirt and flashed me a tight smile that led me to think she was as appalled by the obnoxious display as I was.

I wanted to demand that she rethink her choice of mentor, but it wasn't my place to comment. I was merely a tag-along, and the lady of the manor's lack of acknowledge-ment when we arrived had proved it.

Judith finally sashayed into the room. After moving a view-blocking fake floral display from the coffee table, she sat down opposite us.

"Now," she crooned, alternating glances between the two of us. "Where were we?"

Fiona spoke quickly, probably mindful of being cut off again. "I wanted to let you know that I'm going away for a while." She hooked her arm through mine. "To London, with Jean-Luc."

Judith looked me up and down, but spoke only to Fiona. "This is very unexpected, darling." She didn't sound pleased. "Who is this young man, and why is he stealing you away?"

Holding my tongue was becoming increasingly hard to do. The woman was rude, and despite Fiona's opinion, classless. Taking the high road, I extended my hand across the coffee table and introduced myself.

"Décarie is an unusual name," she exclaimed, weakly meeting my handshake.

"Not if you're French," I replied.

"Tell me something, Jean-Luc," she said, over-enunciating my name. "How does a French boy end up in London?"

Fiona chimed in. "He's studying law at King's College."

The comment was designed to impress. Inexplicably, she was more desperate to have Judith's approval than her own mother's. I could deal with Nellie giving me the third degree – that was her right – but I wasn't going to pander to a society wannabe with no manners.

"Do you have family in London?" she asked, ignoring Fiona completely.

"Yes."

Her bright red lips formed a harsh smile. "*Magnifique.*"

Besides chardonnay, I suspect that was the only French word she knew. I felt the cushion next to me sink as Fiona relaxed her pose. She probably assumed we'd reached the level of polite conversation, but I knew differently. Judith had been slyly grilling me for information since I told her my name, and thanks to Fiona's diary, I knew why.

"Fiona mentioned that you're heavily involved in the charity scene," I said, pushing the process along. "The Sunkiss foundation, I believe."

"You're familiar with it?"

Before I could answer, her housekeeper appeared, carefully balancing a tray of tea. The whole setting rattled as she set it down on the coffee table, and Judith groaned as if she'd broken every piece. "That will be all, Nola."

Again, there was no please or thank you to accompany her comment. I loathed the woman, and was fairly sure that Nola did too.

As Nola exited the room, Fiona picked up where she had left off, pouring three cups of tea as if it was her job to keep the charade going. I wanted to slap her hand away, but held off by turning my attention back to Judith.

"I'm sure you know Jessica Décarie," I said.

"Of course," she crowed. "She's on the board of directors."

Jessica Décarie wasn't merely a board member. She'd founded the Sunkiss foundation ten years earlier while she was married to my father. Jessica was the only one of my three stepmothers that I liked. Unlike the others, she was kind, well-balanced and had an IQ higher than a sack of flour. She was also very self-assured, which meant she was smart enough to put an end to her miserable union with my father after just two years.

"Are you related to her, Jean-Luc?" asked Fiona.

I glanced across at her, frowning slightly. "She was my stepmother for a few years."

"So Thierry is your father?" Judith quizzed.

I swallowed hard, fighting against claiming him. "He is," I finally confirmed.

Judith turned to Fiona. "Running off to London is a decision not to be taken lightly, darling," she said. "I think you should slow things down and take some time to think about it."

Her lightly veiled warning was not unwarranted. My father had a reputation for being one of London's premier scumbags. An endless pot of money enabled him to behave badly on a permanent basis, so it made sense that she thought I was wired the same way. Debauchery, parties and excess were not my thing, but she couldn't have known that.

"I'm a big girl." Fiona shook her head and smiled at me. "I can look after myself, and besides, Jean-Luc will be there."

The sound that escaped Judith's lips could only be described as a whimper. "Oh, dear girl." She stood up and reached for Fiona's hand, pulling her to her feet. "I think we should have a private word in the kitchen."

I said nothing as she led her out of the room, even when Fiona looked back at me wide eyed and confused.

I had no idea what Judith's *private word* entailed, but it was bound to be damaging. Thierry Décarie had stolen, ruined or broken every good thing I'd ever had, and he didn't even need to be in the room to do it.

~

I COULDN'T STAND BEING ALONE IN THAT ROOM A SECOND longer. The gaudy white furniture and plastic floral arrangements were beginning to impair my vision.

In dire need of some fresh air, I slipped out the front door and made my way over to the cab that was parked on the driveway. The driver leant on the open door, smoking a cigarette.

"Is yer lass not coming?" he asked.

"I'm not sure yet." I shrugged. "We'll give her a minute."

"Fine by me." He grinned. "This is the best fare I've had in months."

I didn't need to look at the meter to know that it was costing me a small fortune. At that point I didn't care. It guaranteed a quick escape, and judging by the dour look on Fiona's face when she walked out of the house a few moments later, I was going to need it.

Perhaps realising we needed privacy, the driver sullied the Wiltshire grounds by flicking his cigarette butt into the garden and retreated to his cab.

The gravel driveway crunched beneath Fiona's feet as she approached, and my heart was doing the same thing. We were over before we'd even begun, and it felt dreadful.

"I can take you home if you'd like." I wanted it to sound

like a casual offer but all I conveyed was defeat. "Or anywhere else you want to go."

"I want to go to London," she replied stoically. "Or have you changed your mind?"

I settled my hands in my pockets. "Of course not."

"Judith thinks you'll be a bad influence on me."

"She doesn't know me," I shot back.

Fiona took a step closer, narrowing her pretty navy eyes. "Some might argue that I don't know you either, Jean-Luc."

"I am trying to change that," I told her. "You can ask me anything."

She barely paused for thought. "Judith said your father is famous on the London social scene. Is that true?"

I tried not to grimace. "Infamous would be a more honest assessment."

Not a week went by without some mention of Thierry Décarie in the newspapers. Occasionally, it would be a complimentary piece about some huge donation he'd made to a Children's hospital or a new scholarship program he'd implemented at a local school.

That kind of press alluded to a generous man who should be respected and admired, but it wasn't a true depiction. A more honest appraisal could usually be found in the pages of gossipy rags like *Speak!* magazine or *London Weekly*.

My father was tabloid fodder, and he revelled in the notoriety. Trysts with married socialites, stints in rehab and other despicable antics kept the Décarie name permanently inked across their pages.

He never denied any of it, which meant it was senseless for me to try. "Whatever you heard is probably true," I admitted. "But I am nothing like him."

Her eyebrows lifted. "So he really did shag one of Princess Di's ladies-in-waiting on a flight to Amsterdam?"

I couldn't stop my smile, despite the dire tale. "I haven't heard that one, but I wouldn't put anything past him."

She frowned, which meant she was clearly putting too much thought into it.

"I'm nothing like him, Fiona," I repeated in a whisper. "Nothing."

"I know," she mumbled. "I can't imagine you defiling a lady-in-waiting. You haven't even tried to kiss me since you've been here."

"Not because I don't want to." My tone sounded much too desperate. "I've wanted to kiss you a thousand times."

"You have?"

I dropped my head, inching my face closer to hers. "Perhaps even millions," I amended, brushing the words against her lips.

Fiona slipped her arms around my neck. "You make me giddy, Jean-Luc," she murmured. "And I'm not giving that up for anything."

CHAPTER 6

JEAN-LUC

NO ONE WHO KNEW ME WOULD EVER DESCRIBE ME AS CAREFREE and easy-going, but as the train rolled into Euston station, that's exactly how I felt.

Good things were headed my way – I could feel it. Fiona Black made me happy on a level far above anything I was used to. We'd spent the three-hour journey talking and making plans, and when the words ran out we kissed until they came back.

Her to-do list was a mile long, and everything from window shopping to visiting Buckingham Palace rated a mention. "I didn't get to see it last time I was here," she said wryly. "I got side-tracked by a smooth-talking French geezer."

"Perhaps he thought you were lost," I joked, slipping my arm around her.

"Perhaps I was," she whispered.

The only thing more intense than her cerulean gaze was the feeling of having her lips touch mine. It was like a jolt of electricity, and I wondered how I'd survived for twenty-three years without it.

We barely acknowledged the commotion around us as passengers scrambled to exit the train. I was content to sit there indefinitely, but that plan was cut short when an irate conductor boarded from the platform and told us to get out.

"Before I hose you both down," he threatened.

On the off chance he was serious, we did as we were told, grabbed our luggage and made a beeline for the taxi rank.

~

SILENCE SETTLED BETWEEN US AS THE CAB WEAVED THROUGH the busy city streets. Fiona rested her head against the window, taking in the sights of the place she'd be calling home for the next few weeks.

My thoughts were elsewhere. Of all the subjects we'd touched on, my living arrangements weren't one of them. In a prelude to a difficult conversation, I reached for her hand before breaking the news that I split the rent with a drag queen accountant and a Russian madman. Even to my own ears, it sounded preposterous, but Fiona didn't bat an eyelid.

After taking a short moment to think things through, she asked a very unexpected question. "Do you think they'll like me?"

The notion that she cared enough to worry filled me with absolute joy. "How could they not?" I asked, giving her hand a squeeze. "You make me happy."

And I didn't think they'd ever seen me truly happy before. If nothing else, it would make a nice change.

~

I WASN'T EXPECTING DMITRY TO BE A PART OF THE WELCOME home committee, but it was no surprise when Rhiannon came flouncing out of her room and met us at the door.

It was rehearsal night at the Fizzy Oyster, which meant she was dressed to the nines in an over-the-top show of orange glitter and green feathers.

Perhaps too stunned to move, Fiona stopped dead in her tracks at the sight of her. It was a reaction that Rhiannon was used to. She unabashedly grabbed Fiona's hand and pulled her past me, knocking our luggage over in the process. By the time I righted it and moved it away from the door, they were in the kitchen, and the examination had begun.

Thank God I'd warned Fiona to expect it. She looked calm and interested. I, however, was a nervous wreck.

"I knew you'd be pretty," said Rhiannon, flicking the switch on the kettle. "But I expected a blonde."

"You're pretty too." Fiona's eyes were still wide but her voice was quiet. "Like a sculpted piece of art or something."

Her habit of saying exactly what she was thinking probably didn't always work in her favour, but this time it worked a treat. Rhiannon threw back her head and cackled. "Oh, bless you, sweetheart," she said. "A lot of work goes into looking this fabulous."

"I can see that." She sounded bewildered. "I've never met anyone with green hair before."

"Honey, in my business, it helps to stand out." Rhiannon set a plate of biscuits down on the table. "And pink and blue were taken."

I wasn't too stubborn to see that Rhiannon was going to great lengths to make our guest feel welcome, and as we sat at the small kitchen table drinking tea, I thanked her for it.

"Anything for you, Napoleon."

I frowned hard, but she deflected the silent rebuking by winking at me.

"Why do you call him Napoleon?" Fiona asked, reaching for a chocolate biscuit.

"Well, he's French," she explained. "He's also incredibly

arrogant." Her sly hot pink smile was reserved entirely for me. "And now that you're here, you can confirm my theory that he has other huge attributes besides his ego."

It was a comment designed to shock, and it had the desired effect. Fiona's cheeks flushed red and her eyes flitted in every direction but mine.

"Ignore her," I urged. "She's scandalous."

Fiona quickly changed the subject. "What do you do, Rhiannon?"

It was her wisest play of the day. The quickest way to earn a place in Rhiannon's heart was to show an interest in her theatrical pursuits. Over the next few minutes, Fiona was brought up to speed on every cabaret that had ever been showcased at the Fizzy Oyster night club.

"You should come one night," she suggested. "I'll even wave the cover charge."

If she had smiled and accepted the offer, we probably could've shut afternoon tea down and moved on, but she didn't. Fiona wasn't done questioning her.

"Why do you call yourself Rhiannon?" she asked. "Is it anything to do with the *Fleetwood Mac* song?"

"Yes!" she beamed, flicking the end of her green feather boa. "It's perfect, don't you think?"

Fiona shook her head. "Not really," she replied. "You know that song is about a Welsh witch, right? You're much too glamorous to be a witch."

"Really?" she asked, eyes wide. "I can't have a witch's name. I'm beautiful, for Christ's sake." Outrage made her persona slip, taking her feminine drawl with it. Gordon was at the forefront, and he was pissed. "I'm going to have to change it now. Do you have any idea how hard it is to come up with an original stage name?"

Fiona took a long sip of tea, pondering her question.

"How about you shorten it?" she asked. "You could be Rhianna – Riri for short."

Even though my interest in this conversation was nil, I found myself agreeing with her. "It does sound unique."

"Very unique." Fiona smiled. "What are the chances of ever running across another popstar diva called Rhianna?"

My showgirl flatmate flattened both palms on the table and straightened her pose. "It's settled then," she announced. "I'll have them change the name on my dressing room door. From now on, I shall be known as Riri."

It wasn't like Dmitry to steal her thunder, but as his bedroom door creaked open, all eyes were on him.

"You have had a change in identity?" he asked.

The drag queen formally known as Rhiannon replied with a stiff nod.

He dipped his head at her. "I shall make a note in your file."

Fiona looked both bemused and terrified, and her odd expression intensified as Dmitry approached and ordered her to stand.

He took a small black device out of his pocket and extended the aerial.

"This will alert us to any radio frequency signals that you may be transmitting," he explained.

I slowly shook my head, wishing for nothing more than the ground to open and swallow me whole. "Leave her be, Dmitry," I warned. "She's not bugged."

"We have rules, Jean-Luc." His robotic voice gave no indication of the outrage I knew he was feeling. To Dmitry, inspecting houseguests for listening devices was completely normal behaviour.

"They don't apply to her," I snapped.

"It's okay, Jean-Luc." Fiona slid her chair back and stood,

holding out her arms as if she was about to be frisked by airport security. "Better to be safe than sorry."

I'd momentarily forgotten that Fiona Black was unlike any other. Far from perturbed by his lunacy, she was prepared to humour him to keep the peace.

After a slow and thorough sweep with his detector, Dmitry was placated. "She's clean," he decided, retiring his device to his pocket.

That's when Riri piped up, directing a very sly observation solely at me. "She sure is," she crowed. "Pure as the driven snow."

CHAPTER 7

FIONA

STUDYING PEOPLE IS A HOBBY OF MINE, BUT I'D NEVER COME across subject matter as off-the-wall as Jean-Luc's house-mates in all my life.

He'd warned me that they were odd, but that wasn't a strong enough word to describe a green haired drag queen and a paranoid scientist.

Once Dmitry was satisfied that I had no links to MI5, he disappeared back into his bedroom.

Riri didn't hang around much longer either. After pulling a giant can of Aqua Net hairspray out of her even larger handbag, she announced that she was leaving. "Things to see, people to do," she sang.

It hadn't taken me long to figure out that most of Riri's comments were supposed to incite scandal – much like the rest of her persona. She might've erred on the side of wicked, but she owned it, and I was impressed.

Jean-Luc wasn't as awestruck. "You have no manners, woman."

After dousing her hair in a choking cloud of Aqua Net, Riri aimed the can at him. "And you have too many."

Jean-Luc swatted her hand away. "Go," he ordered. "Before we perish in a haze of chemicals."

Her platform wedges thumped across the wooden floor as she tottered to the door. "Don't wait up for me, kids," she called.

I didn't know what Dmitry got up to while holed up in his room, but it certainly didn't involve loud music or TV. As soon as the front door slammed shut, absolute silence set in.

Jean-Luc looked exhausted, and I wasn't sure if it was the long day we'd had or Riri who'd sapped him of energy. Resting both elbows on the table, he raked his hands through his dark hair. "Would you like me to show you around, *Mademoiselle?*" he asked, lifting his head to look at me.

"I would love that, *Mon-si-err.*"

"*Monsieur,*" he corrected with a chuckle.

"That's what I said – *Mish-err.*"

"No, it's *monsieur.*" He reached across the table for my hand. "Don't pronounce the R."

I gave it one last shot and almost pulled it off. "Better?"

He kissed my fingers. "Perfection," he replied.

My mother had made me promise to remain level-headed and not get caught up in the moment. The problem was, moments with Jean-Luc were flying thick and fast. Once they were all pieced together, there was no doubting that I'd stumbled across something wonderful.

I needed to divert my attention, for both our sakes. I pulled my hand away and glanced around the room. "I guess this is the kitchen?"

"The only one we have," he teased. "Besides the bathroom, this is the only communal area. Needless to say, we spend a lot of time in our rooms."

It was poky but serviceable, and remarkably bright considering the cupboards and countertop were a uniform shade of parsley green. I stood up and walked to the small front window, pushing aside the tatty net curtain to check out the view.

"Is that the Thames?" I asked, catching a glimpse of water in the distance.

"Yes." He replied as if it was no big deal, but I was thrilled to know we were so close to the river.

I spun back to look at him. "Will you take me there?"

A slow smile drifted across his tired face. "Of course."

Dropping my hold on the curtain, I made my way back to the table. "Will you teach me French?"

"Yes, but it might take a while."

"No it won't," I insisted. "I'll have it mastered in six months."

I felt the warmth of his laugh travel right through my body. "I believe you could – but that would involve staying with me for six months."

I took a step back, acutely aware that I'd reverted to being a pushy little cow from Denton. My expression must've hinted toward my chagrin because he quickly spoke again. "You might grow tired of me in a week."

It was impossible to believe that could ever happen, but it was much too early to admit out loud.

"Or you might tire of me," I suggested.

Jean-Luc slid his chair back and moved to stand in front of me. "It's possible," he agreed, tucking my hair behind my ear. "But not very likely given the circumstances."

I was so caught off guard that when I opened my mouth, no words followed. I cleared my throat and tried again. "What circumstances?"

He dropped his head, pressing his lips against the side of my neck. "You're beautiful," he whispered. "And no one ever gets tired of beautiful things."

～

ONCE HE FOCUSED BACK ON TASK, JEAN-LUC'S TOUR TOOK less than a minute. There really wasn't anything to it. Much like the rest of the flat, the small bathroom had seen better days. The pink tiles and fittings were outdated and shabby, but it was clean enough to frequent without wearing flip-flops.

Dmitry and Riri's bedroom doors were shut and I'd already seen the kitchen, which meant there was only one more room to check out.

Jean-Luc hesitated as he reached for his bedroom door handle. "It's nothing spectacular," he warned.

"I'm sure it's fine."

Considering the state of the rest of the home, I was more than a little shocked by what I saw as the door creaked open. The décor was just as tired as the rest of the flat, but the room was huge and the ceiling was high.

"It was originally a living room, I think," Jean-Luc explained. "But the owner commands more rent by touting it as a third bedroom."

It could've been a glorious room. The glimpse of the Thames from the kitchen was miniscule compared to what I could see from the large bay window. It wasn't exactly unin-terrupted, but the low-lying rooftops didn't impede the scene too much.

"I can see boats out there," I mused.

"I'm easily distracted by the view," Jean-Luc replied. "That's why I turned my desk around."

I followed his pointed hand to a chunky wooden desk in the corner. It was covered with an array of papers, a dead modern typewriter and far too many books. I could tell just by looking at them that they exceeded the calibre of my beloved Mills and Boon novels. Anything that was leather bound did not hold tales of romance and ardour.

"You work too hard, Jean-Luc." It was an unqualified

statement to make, but I knew it was true. The rest of the room was practically barren, but his desk was a cluttered mess. He spent too much time there, and it showed.

Jean-Luc dropped his head, chuckling down at the floor. "You might be right," he conceded.

I slowly turned on my heels, coming to a stop when I spotted the bed. Until that moment, I hadn't put much thought into what our sleeping arrangements might be. Now it was all I could think about.

Perhaps sensing my worry, he offered a hasty solution. "I'm happy to take the floor."

My eyes drifted down to the hard oak floor. "What if I'm here six months?"

He shrugged as if it was no big deal. "I'll find a good chiropractor."

"No one's that good, Napoleon."

"Perhaps not," he said looking sheepish. "We can buy another bed."

"And separate them with a bedside table like the Flintstones?" I teased. "My mam will be so pleased."

His low laugh sounded different when tinged with cringing. "Help me out here, Fiona," he pleaded. "I'm trying."

No one was more aware of my virgin status that Jean-Luc. He'd been privy to details in my diary that I hadn't shared with anyone, including Gill and Charlene. I should've been mortified by the thought, but a more adult approach was in order.

"I'm not prudish, and I'm not worried that you'll attack me while I sleep." I stepped closer to him, flattening my palm against his chest. "If you're okay with it, we can share the bed."

It was the sort of compromise that would've sent my mother reeling, but the bed was huge and Jean-Luc was gentlemanly to the extreme.

"I have no objections," he replied.

I turned away and continued my slow wander, but there was nothing else to see. The sparsely furnished room seemed temporary and uninspired, and I couldn't help wondering why he lived there.

"It's not what you were expecting, is it?" he asked. "You look disappointed."

"I don't mean to," I assured him. "I guess I'm just a little confused. It's not very homely."

The man had Vuitton luggage, for crying out loud. I couldn't understand why he was living in a shabby share house with little to no possessions.

Jean-Luc sat down on the edge of the bed. "I don't need it to be homely. It's not my home."

Getting information from him was akin to pulling teeth, and judging by the pained look on his face, Jean-Luc felt the same way. A politer person would've let the subject drop, but I wasn't renowned for good manners.

"Why do you stay here?" I asked.

"It's convenient."

Nothing about sharing a cramped, dingy flat with two people he had nothing in common with seemed convenient or easy – especially considering he could afford much better.

Judith couldn't wait to spill the news that the Décarie family was loaded.

"They have the greenest grass in London *and* France," she'd told me. "It's just too bad that Thierry spends so much time tearing it up."

Maybe he'd cut ties with his family and was going it alone. My mind built a terribly sad picture of him being cast out onto the street with nothing more than a few Pierre Cardin shirts and some fancy luggage.

"Do you see your family often?" My casual tone was

pointless. I was ruthlessly clawing for information, and he knew it.

Jean-Luc pulled in a long breath, and *almost* answered me. "My brother and his wife live in Chelsea." He half-smiled. "My father has a house in Westminster."

I sat down beside him on the bed. "But do you see them?"

"Not often," he conceded. "But that's by choice. We don't have much in common."

"So you're a lone wolf," I announced, slapping my hands on my knees. "Mysteriously living in the shadows."

Lightening the mood was all I could do. If I kept grilling him, he'd likely pass out.

"Holborn is hardly the shadows, Fiona," he said, chuckling. "I'm happy here."

I threw myself back, thumping my head against the mattress. "I'm happy to be here too," I declared making him laugh. "I'm going to learn about London, I'm going to learn French and I'm going to learn about you."

DIARY OF FIONA BLACK

THURSDAY AUGUST 25, 1983

I wonder if there's a ladylike side of the bed.
I chose the left side because it's closest to the window, but what if
that's bad manners? I wanted to call my mam and ask her, but then
I remembered that I was sharing a bed with a boy and she'd likely
bury me for it.
Book of the week: Nowt. No time to read.
Adventure fund: £85.00 (Thanks Mam!)

CHAPTER 8

JEAN-LUC

TRADITIONALLY SPEAKING, AMBITION AND ORGANISATION ARE not the sexiest traits a woman can possess, but I beg to differ. In the first few weeks of her stay, Fiona managed to check off every one of the must-see places on her very long list.

Most of her sightseeing took place while I was at college, and no matter how many times I apologised for the large amount of time she spent alone, she insisted that she didn't mind.

"I wouldn't want you there anyway," she told me. "I get dead weird when I'm close to the palace. My eyes glaze over and I start looking around for corgis to kidnap."

Nothing could've prepared me for the Fiona Black effect. I adored being with her, and when I wasn't, I was thinking about her. She was unintentionally funny, brighter than anyone I'd ever met and far more beautiful than I could ever describe – in English *or* French.

The burden of being a weird, closed-off introvert is a lot easier to carry when you don't feel judged by it, and Fiona never judged anybody. I felt free to drop my guard a little bit, and in turn, we were both figuring out who I was.

$\sim$

AFTER A GRUELLING MORNING OF CLASSES, I ARRIVED HOME just after one. Dmitry was sitting at the kitchen table, cautiously nibbling on a sandwich that he'd dissected into six equal pieces. He looked calm and relaxed, which probably had something to do with the spy-blocking tinfoil hat that he was wearing.

His luncheon companion looked no less odd, nursing a mug of tea with one hand and readjusting her foil bonnet with the other.

"Jean-Luc," Fiona said, sounding truly pleased to see me. "Dmitry was just bringing me up to speed on his technological predictions for the future." Dodging her foil headgear, I leaned down and kissed her cheek. "Did you know that one day we'll all have computers that fit in our pockets?" she asked. "Imagine that!"

I couldn't.

At best, Dmitry's ideas were far-fetched, and as long as he insisted on checking his food for poison and wearing metal on his head, it was impossible to take him seriously.

"Sounds fascinating," I replied, trying my best to sound sincere. "Fi, do you think we could have a word in private?"

"You can speak freely here." Dmitry motioned to Fiona with a stiff nod. "She is completely protected."

Fiona took off her hat and carefully set it down on the table as if it was made of solid gold. "We'll take it to another room, just in case." She gave him a conspiratorial wink and rose to her feet. "Thank you for sharing your ideas with me, Dmitry. I enjoy our chats."

He replied with a stiff nod and a smile that seemed to take great effort. That was the Fiona Black effect in action. Radio frequency signals couldn't penetrate tin foil, but she could cut through it with little more than a few kind words and a wink.

~

My bedroom had undergone some changes of late. My desk was now tidy, but the rest of the space looked like a cross between the women's fiction section of a library and the makeup counter at Fenwick.

Mills and Boon novels scattered the floor on her side of the bed. It wasn't uncommon to find a stray one wedged under my pillow, and I'd endured more than one moment of chagrin when one had dropped out from beneath a stack of my textbooks during class.

The dresser that used to house nothing more spectacular than a lamp and a few law journals was now home to a bewildering array of things that glittered, sparkled or smelled good, and the mirror above was obscured by the haze of hairspray or perfume or whatever else it was that she misfired on a regular basis.

I couldn't decide whether Fiona was a hoarder or if I lived too lightly, but it didn't matter either way. I enjoyed the changes.

"We should get a sofa in here," Fiona suggested, kicking off her shoes and flopping down on the edge of the bed.

My eyes darted around the room. "And put it where?"

"In the drawing room, darling." Her faux aristocratic drawl made me smile. "Where else would one place a red velvet *chaise longue?*"

I crawled across the bed, taking her with me. "You've been practicing," I noted, hauling her in close.

"*Oui, Monsieur,*" she replied. "This French caper is a doddle."

Learning a foreign language is no mean feat, but like

everything Fiona set her mind to, she was making light work of it. Her tenacity impressed me no end, and yet she still maintained that she wasn't the least bit studious.

"Do you really want a chaise in here?" I whispered in her ear.

"No," she replied. "I'll wait until I have a house with a real drawing room. That'd be dead posh."

I would've bought her a chaise if she wanted one. Realistically, I could've bought her a house with a drawing room too, but that was a conversation for another day.

"I got some good news this morning," I said, changing the subject.

"I did too," she replied, fidgeting with a button on my shirt. "But tell me yours first."

"I got my essay back," I said, grinning. "It received high praise."

"The defamation one or the one about vicarious liability?"

Fiona had spent many late nights helping me with both. She'd painstakingly raked her way through my nursery school level notes and woven them into clear, articulate essays that I was proud to submit.

"The defamation one," I replied.

She cupped my cheek in her hand. "I knew you'd nail it."

"Not without you." I turned my head and kissed her palm. "I was close to dropping out a month ago."

"I didn't do anything," she replied. "They were your words. I just tidied them up a bit."

That was an understatement, but I didn't want to argue the point because she was just being polite. My knowledge of the subject matter was good, but no professor in their right mind was going to praise an essay that was riddled with grammatical errors. Fiona had absolutely saved my intellectual skin, whether she'd admit to it or not.

I leaned, murmuring my next words against her soft lips.

"Thank you."

"*Merci beaucoup* to you too, Napoleon," she quipped.

I rolled away, laughing up at the ceiling. "Tell me your news."

"Well, I spoke to my mam this morning."

Any mention of Nellie was bound to mean trouble. Fiona's promise of returning home after two weeks was well and truly broken, and her mother was growing anxious.

"She asked me when I was coming home," she added.

I turned, locking eyes with her. "What did you tell her?"

"The truth," she replied matter-of-factly. "I don't want to go home. I'm happy here with you. She said she's not sending me any more money, and if I want to stay in London I need to stand on my own two feet and get a job."

I swept my fingertips down her arm, settling my hand on her hip. "I'm sorry that she's unhappy," I said quietly. "What are you going to do?"

"I've already done it," she replied. "I got a job."

Grabbing her hand, I levered her to a sitting position. "What do you mean?"

Fiona shrugged as if it was no big deal. "Gordon knows the owner at the cinema on Belgravia Street. He called him and the rest is history." She threw her arms wide. "You're now looking at the Odeon's newest usherette."

Nellie knew the risks when she let Fiona go. Cutting her off financially wasn't going to deter her from making a go of it. Fiona was tenacious and bright enough to stand on her own two feet, and she'd done so at warp speed.

"You are the most amazing creature I've ever known," I mumbled, slowly shaking my head.

Fiona reached, linking her arms around my neck. "I want to stay with you, Jean-Luc. That means I have to keep the ball rolling." She leaned in close and kissed me. "It's onward and upward for us."

CHAPTER 9

FIONA

I'M NOT MUCH OF A MOVIE BUFF, BUT I CAN LIE THROUGH MY teeth when I have to. It was a skill that served me well during my first shift at the cinema.

I was met at the door by a kid called Steven. He looked far too spotty, gangly, and awkward to be the manager, but that was how he introduced himself.

"Do you like movies, Fiona?" he asked.

"Sure." I clutched my Lazar bag for grim death. "Everyone likes movies."

"How about popcorn? Do you like popcorn?"

"Everyone likes popcorn, Steven."

He nodded, seemingly satisfied with my answer. "Do you have popcorn experience?"

"I've eaten popcorn."

He grimaced as if I'd disappointed him. If I had, it was mutual. Steven and I were not going to be lifelong friends, but I wasn't going to give him any trouble. When he suggested that I spend the day working at the refreshment stand, I thanked him and promised to give it my all.

He looked me up and down. "Go upstairs to the office. Cyndi will supply you with a uniform."

Steven grabbed a walkie talkie from his belt and turned away as if that's all it would take to prevent me overhearing the words he mumbled into it. "The new girl is on her way up. She needs a uniform."

After a short pause, his walkie talkie crackled to life. "Is she fat?" asked a voice over the airwaves. "We've got no fat ones in stock."

"No, she's thin," he replied, glancing back to double-check. "That's why I put her on the snack stand."

I was all but convinced that I wasn't going to enjoy my time at the Odeon, but I wasn't going to let it get me down. I hadn't enjoyed working in Mam's shop or housecleaning either, but I'd endured both for a long time.

With no clue where I was going, I headed upstairs and knocked on the first door I came to. After a short moment, it flew open.

"Are you Cyndi?" I asked.

"Yeah." She thrust a pile of clothes at me. "You can change in the bathroom down the hall."

Before I had a chance to utter another word, the door slammed shut.

It was hard not to feel dejected, but I put on a brave face and did as I was told, reminding myself that I needed nothing more from the Odeon than a pay check. I'd find friends elsewhere, and if I didn't, Charlene and Gill were only a phone call away.

Despite the crappy work environment, the day was not a total loss. The refreshment counter was busy, and time passed quickly. Before I knew it, my shift was over and Steven was escorting me to the door.

"You did well," he said. "I'm pleased."

Receiving his approval was borderline creepy. I'd babysat kids older than him, for Christ's sake. "Thanks," I muttered.

"Do you have any questions, Fiona?" he asked.

"Just one." I stopped walking and turned to face him. "Do I get to keep the tights?"

"Excuse me?" In a tell-tale sign that puberty was still on his doorstep, his voice broke. "I'm not sure what you mean."

"Well, these tights are silk," I replied, diverting his attention south by flashing a bit of leg. "I'll be gutted if you make me hand them back."

His face turned beet red. "They're yours," he said, waving both hands as if he was trying to shoo me away. "We have no return policy."

"Excellent," I replied, pulling open the door. "In that case, I'll be back tomorrow."

~

Life in London was different to what I was used to, but I hadn't dropped in from another planet. I was adaptable, and nowhere near as fragile as Jean-Luc thought I was.

I'd already decided to lie and tell him that I had a great first day. There was no need for him to worry, and he worried a lot when it came to my London experience.

My diary was filled with idealistic ramblings of a fairy-tale existence in a far-off land. It made sense that he thought I was pinning all my hopes on finding it here, but I wasn't that naïve. I had no delusions of grandeur. Not every day could be a fanciful mix of sunshine and roses, but I soldiered on because I relished the challenge.

All I wished for was broader horizons and a prince who made my toes curl – and as things stood, both were in reach.

DIARY OF FIONA BLACK

WEDNESDAY SEPTEMBER 7, 1983

There's a movie playing at work called Risky Business.
I think working at the Odeon is risky business.
A group of teenage girls came out of the cinema drooling over that
Tom Cruise bloke. One even kissed the poster of him in the foyer.
Steven yelled at her from the ticket booth. The cheeky mare yelled
back and told him to get a life.
As he was wiping the lipstick smears off Tom's face, he told me
she'd ruined the cinematic experience of others.
I agree with the girl. Steven needs to get a life.
Book of the week: The Knight's Desire
Adventure fund: £82.60

~

It is impossible to throw three random housemates together
and expect that they're going to play nicely all of the time.

I hadn't seen any of them blow their stacks in the month
since I'd been there but as I made my way up the stairs to the
flat, I knew today was the day.

I couldn't make out who was leading the squabble, but as

I walked into the kitchen, I realised it didn't matter. All three of them looked homicidal.

"What's going on?" I set my bag down on the table. "I can hear you from the flippin' stairs."

No one answered me so I set my sights on Gordon. Riri rarely made an appearance before dark, and as much as I missed her zaniness, dealing with Gordon made a nice change. He was quieter, calmer and usually a strong voice of reason.

"It's rent day," he muttered, shooting daggers at his flatmates. "No one wants to do the deed."

I wasn't sure what 'the deed' was, but Dmitry wasted no time in bringing me up to speed. Their landlady lived upstairs on the third floor. She was elderly, eccentric and impossible to deal with.

"She is a maniac," he claimed.

"No she's not," said Jean-Luc. "She's just peculiar."

"It's true," Gordon agreed. "Stepping into her flat is like walking into the Tardis. You're sent back in time, plied with cheap sherry and bored to tears with stories that never happened." He dropped a wad of money down on the table. "The last time I went up to pay the rent, I aged four years."

My eyes drifted to Jean-Luc. "She can't be that bad."

"She can be very trying, Fi," he said diplomatically.

Gordon cut in with a throaty chuckle. "That's not how you described her when she went Mrs Robinson on your French behind."

"She tried to seduce you?" I asked, eyes wide.

He managed to grimace and shrug at the same time. "I fought her off."

Without putting too much thought into it, I snatched the money off the table. "You're all being flippin' babies," I grumbled. "I'll take it to her myself."

"God speed, Fiona," called Dmitry as I made my way to the door.

'Sod off' wasn't usually in my repertoire, but that was the expression that tumbled from my mouth. Perhaps I was channelling Gill, or maybe I'd just reached my idiot limit for the day.

I trudged up the stairs and thumped on the door, much too hard for it to sound anything other than aggressive. I planned to start the conversation with an apology, but when the door opened, the landlady got in first.

"We politely knock with our knuckles, not our boots," she chided. "We're not farm animals."

"I'm… I'm sorry," I stammered.

Although I probably sounded terrified, fear hadn't interrupted my speech. I was gobsmacked at the sight of her, and struggling to function as a result. Dmitry had painted the picture of a feeble old woman, but this lady was nothing of the sort.

My eyes shamelessly travelled from her head to her feet as I took it all in. The only thing more fabulous than her long black dress and blood red lipstick was the white mink stole that was draped around her shoulders.

"Are you quite finished, darling?"

I was now certain that 'darling' was my favourite word. One day I hoped to be qualified to use it myself, but until then I was content to leave it to the experts – and this lady was a pro.

She touched her lips with the opera length black cigarette holder she had balanced between her fingers, and deeply inhaled. "Staring is the height of rudeness." The words got caught in the ring of smoke she directed at the ceiling, which left me feeling one part awed, and one part queasy.

"I'm just here to pay the rent for flat number four." I reached into my pocket for the money. "I think it's all here."

Her eyes drifted to the bundle of cash in my hand, but she made no attempt to take it from me. "What's your name, darling?"

"Fiona Black," I replied.

"Do you know who I am, Fiona Black?" she asked.

I shook my head, telling her no.

"I am Lady Kitty DeVille," she announced with reverence.

My mouth hijacked my brain and made it say foolish things. "Any relation to Cruella?" I asked.

If Kitty was outraged, she didn't let on. "I'm not a fan of Dalmatians, nor am I cruel."

"Of course not," I mumbled down at the floor. An awkward silence set in until I worked up the courage to speak again. "Do you always wear mink during the day?"

"I have a dinner engagement at seven," she replied. "Preparedness is the key."

Getting dressed three hours beforehand seemed like overkill to me, but I said no more. Instead, I waved the rent money at her again.

Finally, she snatched it from my hand. "Tell the young men in number four that I appreciate their prompt payment."

"I will," I replied.

Lady Kitty took a step forward and began to close the door. "Come back and visit me again some time, Miss Black."

"I will," I repeated.

Probably next month when the rent is due again, I didn't add.

Having the door closed in my face didn't bother me in the slightest. There was a skip in my step as I leapt down the stairs, and it was all thanks to the fabulous Lady Kitty DeVille.

CHAPTER 10

JEAN-LUC

IT WAS A RELIEF TO HEAR THE FRONT DOOR OPEN. FIONA couldn't have been gone more than a few minutes, but better than anyone I knew that was more than enough time for Lady Kitty to scar her for life.

Dmitry and Gordon had retreated to their rooms so by the time she rounded the doorway, I was the last man standing.

Her mood hadn't been great when she left, but there was no hint of indignation on her face now. If anything, she was beaming. "Lady Kitty thanks you for your prompt payment." She dipped her head and curtsied. "And she hopes to see you soon."

As soon as she was in reach, I took her in my arms. "I can't see that happening," I replied, enjoying the wonderful sensation of her warm laugh against my chest. "The woman frightens me."

Fiona lifted her head to look at me. "I think she's the most glamorous woman I've ever met."

"You said the same thing about Judith," I reminded her.

Her smile was wry. "Judith who?"

It was hard to pinpoint exactly what Fiona found so fascinating about women of polite society, especially considering that most were rarely polite. In my opinion, her own mother was a much better role model but I knew she wouldn't appreciate hearing it. Instead, I changed the subject and asked if she'd enjoyed her day at work.

"How could I not?" Fiona took a step back sweeping her hands up and down her body as she showcased her uniform. "I got a new pair of tights."

I took her face in my hands, pressing my smile against her lips. "Have I told you how much I enjoy a woman in uniform?" I murmured.

"No," she replied. "But I think we should go to our room and discuss it some more in private. I know Dmitry is listening."

"I am not the enemy," he called from his bedroom. "Your government poses far more of a threat than I do."

"Told you," she whispered, pulling me toward the door.

As soon as we were on the other side, I kicked it shut with my foot. "This place is a madhouse," I muttered under my breath.

How the poor girl endured it was beyond me. Fiona had dealt with nothing but craziness since she'd arrived. Between the antics of Dmitry, Riri and now Kitty DeVille, she was surely close to breaking point.

She sat down on the edge of the bed and kicked off her shoes. "I happen to like this madhouse."

I wasn't about to question why. I asked far too many questions when it came to her wellbeing, which was unnecessary and annoying to both of us. Fiona was more than capable of keeping her own happiness in check. If something wasn't working out, she fixed it. That was how she operated.

Her eyes held my gaze as I wandered over to the bed. "I happen to like you," I murmured.

My whole body ignited when she reached out and pulled me down on top of her. I gently kissed her, feeling the familiar scorch of her touch hit me hard in the chest.

Fiona Black was the best lover I'd never had.

We'd shared a bed for over a month, and our time wasn't always spent keeping a respectful distance, but there was a line that never got crossed and the slow burn was gradually killing me. Pulling away from her was a form of self-preservation, and she knew it.

I rolled to the side and let out a long breath. Fiona shifted, resting her head on my chest. "If our life together was a romance novel, what chapter would we be up to?" she asked.

I stared up at the water mark on the ceiling, absently stroking her back. "Four," I decided.

"That's fair," she replied. "I was thinking three, but I probably read slower than you do."

I kissed the top of her head. "We have all the time in the world."

"Jean-Luc, what if you get bored of waiting?"

Boredom wasn't the issue. It was the sheer physical frustration that was doing me in, but explaining it was impossible. "I promise you, I respect your decision to wait."

She touched my cheek and turned my head toward her. "I want more than your body, you know."

Every woman I'd ever been with had wanted more than my body, but Fiona wasn't talking about money. She wasn't hinting at lavish gifts of diamonds and jewels either. All she wanted was the opportunity to know me as well as I knew her, and I wasn't sure how to give it to her.

∾

I have never been a fan of team sports, and after joining

the rowing team during my first year at university, I still wasn't a fan.

But I did love rowing.

There's something very intense about propelling a boat through the water using nothing more than the power of your body. It takes a high degree of strength, endurance and mental toughness, and on days when I was convinced that I lacked those traits, rowing proved me wrong.

When my grades started to slip, I made the decision to give up my place on the team in favour of extra study. The rest of the crew were hardly devastated. Before the day was out, they'd replaced me with someone else and I hadn't heard a word from any of them since.

Being shunned didn't come as any great shock. I wasn't friends with any of them, and it didn't take a genius to work out that they weren't particularly fond of me either.

I fell off their social radar in an instant, but someone must have neglected to cut me from their mailing list. When one of their trademark blue envelopes turned up amongst my mail, I tossed it onto my desk without even opening it. By the time Fiona came across it a few days later, I'd all but forgotten it was there.

"What's this about?" she asked, waving it at me.

I shrugged. "It's nothing important."

Eyes narrowed, she glared at the envelope in her hand as if she was trying to burn a hole through it. "It looks important."

"It's not," I assured her. "Read it if you want to."

Without a moment of reluctance, she ripped it open. "The Royal Rowing Society celebrates its Annual Regatta Day on Saturday the twenty-fourth of September," she announced in a pompous English brogue. "You are cordially invited to grace the occasion with your benign presence."

She continued to stare at the page long after the words

had run out. I stared at her instead, trying to figure out what she'd make of such a ridiculously formal note.

Finally, she looked across at me. "Benign presence?" she asked. "Like a tumour?"

I folded my arms, directing my dark chuckle at the floor-boards. "A person of benign presence has a kind and gentle disposition," I explained. "It's terribly archaic, but they pride themselves on tradition."

"I see," she replied. "So what happens on Regatta Day?"

"Well, the men race their boats down the river while the women sit on the banks and watch. There are usually trophy presentations and speeches afterwards."

Fiona stepped forward, uncrossed my arms and slipped her arms around my middle. I should've known that my breakdown of events wasn't nearly detailed enough to mollify her. She had questions, and I wasn't free to leave until I answered them.

"Do the women drink champagne?" she asked.

"Probably."

"And do they wear wide brim hats and big sunglasses?"

"I have no idea, Fiona."

"I bet they flippin' do," she insisted. "Eating cucumber sandwiches on the banks of the Thames while their men compete." She let out a wistful sigh. "Dead posh, isn't it?"

"Cucumber sandwiches?" I asked, completely mystified. "I never said anything about cucumber sandwiches."

"You didn't have to," she replied. "They're all the rage at upper-class soirees."

I don't know what image she was conjuring up in her pretty brain, but a rowing regatta could hardly be described as an upper-class soiree. "It's not a night out at the opera, Fi," I reminded her. "It's just a pretentious event organised by a committee of insipid socialites who know nothing about the sport."

She narrowed her eyes. "You don't speak highly of your people, Jean-Luc."

I slowly shook my head, smiling because her fake haughty accent gave me no choice. "They're not *my* people, Fiona."

"Embossed invitations don't lie, *Monsieur*," she said, motioning toward my desk with a nod.

Breaking her gaze, I looked up at the ceiling and let out a long sigh. "Do you really want to go?"

I already knew the answer, but I waited to hear it out loud. "Of course I flippin' do," she replied. "I'd love to meet your people."

CHAPTER 11

FIONA

It would've pained my mother to know that there wasn't much I missed about being away from home. I was enjoying my newfound freedom and independence, and the lovely infusion of romance in my life made me wonder why I'd wasted so long making do without it.

The only thing I truly missed were girly chats with Charlene and Gill, but it was a gap that could be filled by a phone call home or spending time with Riri.

My friendship with the glitzy showgirl was decidedly unbalanced. I was in awe of her very existence. Riri was intriguing and fascinating, and she never took offence when I asked her intrusive or stupid questions.

I got the impression that she found me mildly annoying, but the urge to shoo me away like a fly never quite took hold, even when I muscled in on her epic makeup sessions.

The dressing table in her bedroom reminded me of the setup in Becky Cox's hair salon. Nine bright bulbs framed the mirror, casting a harsh light that no one could possibly look good under.

Riri sat on a low stool, carefully studying the huge spread

of makeup that was laid out in front of her. "Plum or apricot blush tonight?" she asked.

I shrugged, not caring either way. "Both sound equally fruity."

It was a mortifying slip of the tongue that sucked the air right out of my lungs. Silence hung between us with the weight of a brick until I eventually managed to find my voice. "Riri, I – I'm so sorry," I stammered. "Sometimes my mouth kicks into gear before my brain."

She stared at me through the mirror, looking more perplexed than incensed. "Sweetheart, I've been called far worse than fruity in my time," she replied.

That should've been the end of it, but I was horrified and determined to keep babbling. "I warned Jean-Luc that I had no clue what I'm doing." I sounded as defeated as I felt. "I'm always saying or doing something inappropriate."

Riri's heavy eyebrows knitted together as she frowned. "Says who?" she asked. "Napoleon?"

"He'd never admit to it, but I think that's why he doesn't want to take me to the regatta on Saturday."

Swish social events like that were not my scene and he knew it. There was every chance that I'd unwittingly behave badly, and I couldn't blame Jean-Luc for wanting no part of it.

"He told you that?" she asked, eyes wide.

I shook my head, telling her no. "He's much too polite to say anything. I just put two and two together."

Riri picked up a huge brush and roughly dusted it across her face as if she was trying to erase the skin on her cheeks. "Why would the fool agree to take you if he feels that way?"

"Because he likes me," I replied, shrugging. "I guess I'm a work in progress."

Everything on the dressing table rattled as she tossed the brush aside. "Let me tell you something, Fiona," she said sternly. "From one queen to another." Riri spun on the stool to face me. "No one is superior to you, least of all Jean-Bloody-Luc."

The problem was, I was convinced that I was superior to myself, and that had nothing to do with Jean-Luc. My princess tendencies had been firmly set in place long before I met him.

"In my head, I'm royalty." I spoke with a touch of theatre in my voice. "Full of airs and graces that I don't really have."

"In my head, I'm Tina-Bloody-Turner," she said, finally breaking a smile. "And don't get me started on the parts of her that I don't have."

My eyes drifted to the makeup on the dresser. "It doesn't feel dishonest though, does it?" I asked. "It's who you are and you shouldn't be judged for it."

Breaking into high society wasn't a conventional dream, but impersonating Tina Turner while belting out show tunes at the Fizzy Oyster wasn't exactly orthodox either.

"I'm not judging you," she insisted. "But money and good manners don't make you fabulous."

"I know that, Riri."

She picked up a hairbrush and pointed it at me like a wand. "And if Napoleon ever makes you feel otherwise, dump his French arse."

DIARY OF FIONA BLACK

SUNDAY SEPTEMBER 11, 1983

Riri's makeup is so flippin thick that it whites out her eyebrows.
When I asked if she sweats while she's on stage, she said yes.
In her words, she gets hotter than a whore in church.
And to think I was worried about offending her.......
Book of the week: Capturing His Heart
Adventure Fund: £103.30

CHAPTER 12

JEAN-LUC

IF ANYONE WOULD BENEFIT FROM A CRASH COURSE IN sensitivity and tact, it was probably me. But for now, it was left to Gordon to pull me aside and remind me that being oblivious is no excuse for poor behaviour.

"Fiona is under the impression that you're somehow embarrassed by her behaviour at social gatherings," he announced. "I sincerely hope she's mistaken."

No matter how many times I repeated the accusation in my head, I couldn't make it stick. "Gordon, I have no idea what you're talking about. There is nothing that Fiona could ever say or do that would embarrass me."

"I'm talking about the rowing regatta," he snapped. "She said you don't want to take her."

It was hard to imagine any such conversation taking place, but only because I was hearing about it from Gordon. Riri was Fiona's confidante, and when face to face with the straight-laced accountant, I had to constantly remind myself that they were one and the same.

"She's right. I *don't* want to take her," I admitted, mindlessly stirring my coffee. "But only because it will be a boring waste of a Saturday afternoon."

My aversion to attending pomp events wasn't limited to the regatta. I loathed any gathering that called for fake minutiae and plastic smiles.

Seemingly satisfied with my explanation, Gordon's frown slipped. He took a bite of toast, and then dropped it back on the plate. "You should be doing all you can to impress this girl," he said, dusting his hands together. "She's fabulous and you should want to keep her."

"She is and I do."

It was an admission that I never intended to make out loud, but it was honest, which somehow made it less painful.

Gordon leaned, checking out his reflection in the kettle. "That's just not the vibe you're putting out there, Jean-Luc."

I frowned, more confused than ever. "I have a vibe?"

"Of course you do." He grabbed his briefcase off the table and let out a hard chuckle. "It's serious, brooding and sulky."

I wasn't surprised by his harsh assessment, but hearing it out loud bothered me more than I expected it would. "Charming," I muttered sarcastically.

Gordon slapped his hand down on my shoulder. "Chin up, Napoleon," he quipped. "Some of us enjoy the angsty French persona."

When all was said and done, I didn't care what sort of vibe I presented to my flatmates, but Fiona's opinion did matter, and if Gordon was correct she thought I was an elitist snob who was ashamed to be seen with her.

"I will set the record straight with Fiona," I said formally.

"You do that," he replied, heading for the door. "Lord knows she deserves more than the crooked path you've been leading her down so far."

~

When our schedules allowed, Fiona and I spent her half-hour break eating lunch in the square down the road from the cinema. We usually grabbed a quick bite at a nearby café but today she had other plans.

"I made us lunch," she proudly announced.

It was a statement that drove fear into my heart. Fiona was a woman of many talents, but none of them were food related. Her culinary efforts were so appalling that my housemates had called a secret meeting in her absence and made me promise to keep her out of the kitchen.

"She'll kill us all," warned Dmitry. "And no one will believe it was accidental."

Gordon had been a little more diplomatic. "The girl can burn water, Jean-Luc," he'd told me. "You mustn't encourage the madness."

Since then, I'd managed to keep her a safe distance from the stove but today, there was no escape.

Fiona thrust a poorly wrapped sandwich at me. "It's cucumber," she said. "You'll love it."

I wanted to break the news that no one in their right mind would love it, but I held my tongue. My mission for the day was to convince her that I wasn't a highbrow jerk, and bursting her cucumber bubble would've been counterproductive.

"I'm sure it's wonderful," I replied, taking it from her.

"You look dead worried, Jean-Luc." Her soft laugh floated toward me. "You don't have to eat it if you don't want to."

The wooden bench seat creaked as I shifted, highlighting my unease. "I do have something on my mind," I confessed. "But it's nothing to do with lunch."

Fiona placed her sandwich on her lap and gingerly unwrapped it. "Tell me," she urged.

"Gordon cornered me this morning." I could feel the tension taking hold as I spoke, which wasn't a promising start. "He mentioned that the two of you have been discussing my lack of enthusiasm regarding the regatta. I just want to make sure you understand why I'm less than eager to attend."

At first, I couldn't decide whether she looked angry or confused, but the act of thumping her sandwich down on her lap quickly helped me decide. She was furious, and I wasn't sure why.

"It took you a bucket load of words to tell me that you've been gossiping about me?" she growled. "With Gordon no less!"

Now I was confused.

"Fi, you told him – "

"I didn't tell *him* anything," she fiercely cut in. "I spoke to Riri, and she's a lot better at keeping secrets than him."

I leaned back on the seat, dumbfounded. After a long pause, I took a shot at pointing out the obvious. "They're the same – "

"I know they're the flippin' same person, Jean-Luc," she snapped. "But it was a private conversation that you were never meant to hear about."

"So you're mad at both of them?" I teased.

Fiona pursed her lips, unsuccessfully trying to hide her smile. "Furious," she replied. "And embarrassed."

I slipped my arm behind her, resting it on the back of the seat. "I never want you to feel that way," I replied. "My anti-social predispositions have nothing to do with you."

"No need to throw the dictionary at me again, Jean-Luc." She dropped her head and chuckled. "Let's just accept that you're a wanker and move on."

I could accept the title of wanker without question, but nothing had been explained or resolved, which meant we were still on the proverbial crooked path that Gordon had warned me about. I had little choice but to forge ahead with the awkward conversation, for both our sakes.

"I know that you're intrigued by privilege and wealth," I began. "And there's nothing wrong with that."

"There is when you say it like that," she muttered.

"I don't know how else to say it, Fiona."

"In a way that makes me sound a little less like a try-hard gold digger would be good."

The notion of her being a money-grubber was preposterous. It was the blueblood lifestyle that held her fascination. If Kitty DeVille and Judith Wiltshire had been paupers, she still would've been smitten. Fiona was enchanted by their fur coats, haughty accents and big sunglasses, not the money in their pockets.

I set my lunch down on the bench beside me and reached for her hand. "Tell me why you want to go to the regatta."

And then I'll tell you why I don't, I silently added.

Fiona let out a wistful sigh. "You'll think I'm silly."

"I promise I won't."

"I just want to see how they tick, Jean-Luc," she replied. "I want to study them up close and learn everything."

I couldn't help but smile. I had always imagined the girl of my dreams to be ambitious, well-read and scholarly. Fiona Black was all those things without even realising it.

"I want to know the proper way to hold a wine glass." She daintily held up her sandwich as if it was made of lead crystal. "And I want to know how to gracefully walk down stairs."

"Anything else?" I asked, fighting the urge to kiss her to death.

"The lesson plan is long, my friend," she replied, flashing me a lovely grin. "I also want to know how to gracefully walk down stairs while holding a wine glass."

Better than anyone, I knew that British society was a tough nut to crack. You do not rise to your station; you are born into it. And even then, maintaining your position is as perilous as sitting on a high-rise window ledge. One misstep and you're banished for life, and therein lies the rub. The Décaries had plunged headfirst to the ground years ago.

"Fi, I know how badly you want the society experience, but entering that realm on my arm is no prize ticket," I quietly explained. "My name is mud and I'm treated accordingly."

I'd experienced the full gamut of slighting in my time, ranging from snide whispers to the iciest of cold shoulders. It bordered on brutal, and there was no way I'd willingly subject Fiona to it.

"Attending that regatta will be like sending you to a gunfight without a weapon," I added gravely. "I don't want you to get hurt."

She nodded but disappointment marred her sweet face. "This is all because of your father?" she asked.

"Everything begins and ends with Thierry." My voice was pure acid. "He's a foolish buffoon who has systematically managed to burn every bridge in town."

Her eyes drifted from mine as she focused her attention on the view in front of her. People were making the most of the midday sun, milling around while they chatted, or eating lunch on the bench seats that lined the square. It was a completely ordinary scene that didn't match the extraordinary conversation we were having.

"How did he become wealthy?" Fiona glanced at me only briefly. "What does he do for a job?"

My father had never worked a day in his life, which was one of the many reasons why I had no respect for the man. It was a luxury afforded to him by previous generations of Décaries who *were* exceptionally industrious.

"He lives off an inheritance," I explained. "Once in a while he opens a fancy night club or a bar, but once the hype dies down, the doors shut for good and he moves onto something else."

I hated the tinge of shame in my voice because it didn't belong to me. I was trying my hardest to make something of myself, and being tied to him felt like a noose around my neck.

"Was he always hopeless?" Fiona asked.

"He went off the rails after my mother died. My brother and I could go months without seeing him. We stayed in Marseille and he took off to London."

She whipped her head to look at me, boring into me with concerned blue eyes. "You were just left to fend for yourselves?"

"Not quite," I replied, half-smiling. "We had nannies and cooks and whatever else we needed to survive. When we got older, he sent us off to boarding school. It wasn't a completely miserable existence."

If anything, we relished the peace of not having to deal with the influx of random women and his all night benders, but that was more information than I was willing to share. The horrified look on her face led me to think she already considered me to be damaged goods.

"I'm sorry, Jean-Luc," Fiona whispered. "That must've been really tough."

I pulled in a long breath. "Don't feel sorry for me, Fi," I said stoically. "I'm on the right track."

"Why didn't you just stay in France?" She pulled a crust off her sandwich and tossed it to a nearby pigeon. "Thierry could've continued raising hell and you'd never have been stuck dealing with the fallout."

"I wanted to attend university here," I replied. "But if I ever manage to graduate, I'll go home."

She flashed me a lovely smile. "Of course you'll graduate."

I loved that she had such faith in me. Perhaps that meant

that I loved her, but that was a thought for another day. For now, I was content knowing that I'd managed to straighten our crooked road a little bit.

I hadn't painted the full picture of my life, but the important part was that I felt like I could. I wanted her to know everything about me and I wanted to give her everything that I had. And that was the wonderment of Fiona Black.

CHAPTER 13

FIONA

I HAD SPENT MY ENTIRE LIFE STUCK IN A PLACE CALLED NEVER land, which is a state of mind brought on by the feeling that no matter what I had to offer the world, it would never be enough. The list of things I'd never be was long:

Worldly enough.

Polite enough.

Good enough.

Never enough anything.

And as if that wasn't frustrating enough, my ex-fiancé's parting shot was a complaint that I was *too* much.

Pushy.

Bossy.

One-track.

Too everything.

I had no idea where I fit in, and I dealt with those confusing insecurities by trying to better myself and change who I was. It occurred to me that Jean-Luc was doing the same thing.

After weeks of trying to crack his tough armour, he broke it himself. Getting an insight into his family life gave me a better understanding of who he was and why he was so incredibly guarded.

It also made me realise that my idealistic views on the lifestyles of the rich and privileged were seriously skewed. In my mind, designer clothes and champagne didn't go with dysfunction and chaos. The people who ran with that crowd were supposed to be above all that, but Thierry Décarie sounded no more refined than Mandy Brewer and her high-top sneakers.

For the first time ever, I wanted no part of it.

Attending the regatta was out of the question, but the wannabe socialite living in my brain couldn't let us bail without notice.

While Jean-Luc sat at his desk doing whatever it is that Jean-Luc does while studying, I penned a letter to the Royal Rowing Society.

"How does this sound?" I asked.

Jean-Luc swivelled his chair to face me.

"I appreciate your gracious invitation to the annual rowing regatta." The posh princess voice I adopted was so well practiced that it barely took effort. "Unfortunately I already have another engagement that day and will be unable to attend. May you enjoy a wonderful event… you gossipy, nasty bitches."

Jean-Luc's wonderful deep laugh filled the room. "I think it's perfect," he replied. "I also think it'll guarantee my omission from the guest list next year."

"It's no loss." I tossed the letter aside and scrambled off the bed. "We'll be busy then too."

As soon as I was in reach, he pulled me down onto his lap. "Now that we have no plans for Saturday, we should do something special – just the two of us," he suggested.

I linked my arm around his neck and smiled. "Like what?"

His warm brown eyes held mine for an eternity. "Leave the details to me," he murmured. "I'll figure something out."

"Something involving moonlight, seduction and bewitchery?"

Jean-Luc's hand slipped underneath my shirt. "What is the correct order of play?" he asked, absently drawing circles on my back. "Bewitchery then seduction, or is it the other way around?"

I wasn't even sure what bewitchery was. All I knew was that it was mentioned four times in one chapter of my latest read, *Capturing His Heart,* and it sounded dead romantic.

"I'll leave that up to you." My casual tone implied that I didn't care either way, but nothing could be further from the truth. I wanted to be seduced by this man, and if bewitchery was part of the process, I was up for that too.

Jean-Luc dipped his head, pressing his lips against mine. "Prepare to be swept off your feet, *Mademoiselle* Black," he whispered.

My whole body shuddered, and it had little to do with the way he was touching me. It was the look he gave as he said them that set me on fire. In his eyes, I wasn't some pushy cow from Denton. I *was* good enough and I promised never to let myself forget that I had been from the minute we met.

DIARY OF FIONA BLACK

MONDAY SEPTEMBER 12, 1983

The heroine in my latest read was seduced by a man called Miklos.
It all went down under the blazing sun on a deserted beach near a
grove of palm trees.
For a few reasons, it's the most unromantic scene I've ever read.
First, there's nothing sexy about having your knickers fill
with sand.
And the blazing heat and palm tree scenario would've had her
sweating cobs and dodging coconuts.
Sod that!!
Tomorrow I'm going to tell Jean-Luc that I don't like the beach.
Book Of The Week: Capturing His Heart
Adventure Fund: £100.12

CHAPTER 14

JEAN-LUC

MY PLANS FOR SATURDAY NIGHT INVOLVED PULLING OUT ALL the stops – and that involved a trip to one particular boutique on King's Road.

Melinda Lazar Designs was an upmarket boutique frequented by the rich, famous and infamous. Modern silver mannequins were strategically posed in the large arched windows, showcasing the latest collection of clothes, bags and shoes. It was high-end, exclusive and just as pompous as the woman who designed them.

It wasn't a place I took any joy in visiting, but today I was a man on a mission. After psyching myself up with a few deep breaths, I pushed on the heavy glass door.

A girl dressed in a red jumpsuit and ridiculously high heels tapped her way across the tiled floor to greet me. "Welcome to the House Of Lazar." Her arms were stretched wide as if she was hoping for a hug. "What can I help you with today?"

I was saved from having to reply when another woman chimed in from behind the counter. "I doubt he can be helped at all. I tried for years to help the ungrateful little snot."

And there she was – Melinda Lazar – step-mother number one.

"Hello, Mel." My voice was completely flat. "Still vicious, I see."

I hung by the door as she sauntered toward me. "What are you doing here, Jean-Luc?"

I kept her hanging for an answer while I shamelessly studied the woman who'd stepped into my mother's shoes less than a year after her passing. I hadn't seen her in a long time, but other than her hair colour, nothing had changed. When I knew her, she was platinum blonde, mean and wore a permanent scowl to prove it. She was sporting a jet black do these days, but the scowl remained.

"I'm here to shop, actually," I replied. "I bet you didn't see that coming."

She threw her head back and cackled – and that obnoxious manoeuvre hadn't changed either. It was still grating. "For what?" she asked. "Manners and a back bone?"

Perhaps realising that her overenthusiastic sales pitch would be wasted on me, the girl in red quickly retreated, slipping behind a curtain and out of view. Melinda didn't seem to notice. She was too busy trying to damage me with a baleful glare.

"I doubt I'd find either of those here," I casually replied.

She gave up trying to stare me down and turned away, aimlessly wandering around the store. "I never liked you," she spat. "You were such a needy, whiny child."

I expect that had something to do with the fact that my mother had died and my father wouldn't give me the time of day, but I felt no need to enlighten her. At five-years-old, I tried hard to work my way into her good graces, but now that I was grown, I didn't give a damn what she thought of me.

"Can we forget about reminiscing?" I asked, glancing at a display of purses near the counter. "It's tiresome. I'm here to shop, nothing more."

I could think of a hundred places I'd rather be dropping money, but as fate would have it, Mel Lazar was Fiona's favourite designer.

Perhaps realising I was above being rattled, she dropped the bitterness from her tone. "Who are you shopping for?" she asked.

"My girlfriend."

Callous glee filled her eyes. "Who's the unlucky lady?"

"No one you'd know." I picked up a black sequined purse and held it out to her. "She'd probably like this one."

Melinda huffed out a sharp laugh. "Of course she would. There's not a woman alive who doesn't appreciate my designs."

I shook my head, trying to shift the aggravation that was seeping into my brain. "Humble as ever," I muttered.

Mel snatched the bag from my grasp. "I don't need to be humble, darling. And I have the bank account to prove it."

"Oh yes," I crowed. "Still receiving the alimony, I presume?"

Her sour expression led me to think that she was. Being married to my father for less than five years had been hugely profitable for her. He'd probably paid for her high-end store and everything in it a hundred times over.

"Thierry has always been very generous to me," she replied through gritted teeth. "We have much love for each other."

The derisive laugh that tumbled from my mouth sounded like a snort. "You have good attorneys," I reminded her. "Let's be honest."

Her union with my father had ended abruptly when she caught him in bed with her personal assistant. Melinda lawyered up, went for the throat and won an unprecedented settlement that my father ranted about for the next ten years.

"The most expensive divorce in Britain," I announced with a touch of theatre in my voice. "That was the headline, wasn't it?"

She grinned. "*London Weekly* is nothing if not sensational."

I shook my head. "Both of you deserve each other."

"That's what I keep telling him," she replied. "But Thierry refuses to revisit old ground."

"You'd take him back?" I asked incredulously.

"I do," she told me. "Every Wednesday night."

I swallowed hard. It was all I could do to stop myself from throwing up. I had no idea they were back in contact, but it wasn't really surprising. My father had wronged just about every woman in London in one way or another. His options when it came to warming his bed at night were surely becoming limited.

I pointed at the bag in her hand. "Just ring up the sale, Mel," I said listlessly. "Then I can get out of here and shower."

Her whole face changed as her expression softened, making her almost look human. "Listen, Jean-Luc," she glanced at the purse in her hand, "I know things are strained between you and your father, but there shouldn't be animosity between us."

"I don't feel animosity toward you, Melinda," I replied. "I feel nothing for you."

She continued as if I hadn't spoken. "Send your girlfriend to me. I could make her a dress to go with the bag. Then you could spoil her with dinner somewhere special – The Copper Grove perhaps."

Accepting her offer seemed like the dumbest idea on

earth, but I knew for Fiona, it would be a dream come true. Perhaps that's why I was considering it.

"You can make the reservation for me." I was only half-joking. "A table for two on Saturday night."

She grinned. "You don't think you'd get in using your own name?"

"I'm certain I wouldn't," I replied.

My children and grandchildren would probably have a hard time getting a table there. Thanks to my father's debauchery, it was one of the many London haunts that Décaries were not welcome at. Rumour has it that he was physically removed from the building after a drunken tantrum. Just thinking about it made me cringe.

Melinda knew exactly what I was up against where Thierry was concerned. Maybe that's why she took pity on me and agreed to make the call on my behalf.

"No one should be banished from The Copper Grove," she said, walking toward the counter. "Everyone should eat there at least once, even poor little rich boys like you."

I didn't bite back because she picked up the phone. Instead, I settled my hands in my pockets and listened as the nastiest ghost from my past paid me a huge favour and booked us a table at the most exclusive restaurant in London.

"Done," she announced, hanging up. "Now you have no excuse not to send your girl to me. She needs a spectacular dress to wear."

I wasn't sure if I'd been backed into a corner or if I'd put myself there. Either way, the result was the same. I'd handed Fiona to her on a platter.

"I really like this girl, Melinda," I told her. "If you so much as look at her the wrong way I'll –"

"You'll what, Jean-Luc?" she interrupted. "The waiting list to be dressed by me is a mile long. I'm offering you the opportunity to cut in line. I'm sure your little girlfriend would appreciate the gesture. Why can't you?"

My eyes darted around the boutique. There was diamantes, lace and silk for as far as the eye could see. Of course Fiona would appreciate it.

"Fine," I relented. "Just try and be nice for a change. She doesn't deserve your venom."

CHAPTER 15

FIONA

The Copper Grove is one of the most elite restaurants in London. The only reason I knew of its existence is because I'd read about it in a copy of *London Style* magazine that I found wedged under the drink machine at work.

I added it to my long list of places to visit before I die and then promptly forgot about it until Jean-Luc surprised me with the news that he'd made reservations there for Saturday night.

"You don't look pleased," he said worriedly.

Perhaps the stunned look on my face had something to do with it. "I am," I assured him. "I'm just.... surprised. How on earth did you manage to get us in?"

According to *London Style*, it was so exclusive that getting in was akin to winning the lottery. I didn't know if it was the food or clientele that made it such a hot ticket – both were described as 'unashamedly decadent.'

Jean-Luc set his book bag down on the table. "I have a few connections." He wiggled his eyebrows. "I'm not a total leper."

I jumped out of my seat and practically flung myself at

him, wrapping my arms tightly around his neck while I kissed him over and over. "I'm so excited!" I exclaimed. "I've never been anywhere that grand before."

Jean-Luc held me tighter, which seemed more tactical than romantic. I was in danger of kissing the skin off his face by that point. "There's more," he said, reaching for his bag with his free hand.

When he presented me with a gift box, I nearly fainted. "Is this Melinda Lazar?" I already knew the answer. The silver logo on the ribbon holding it together was a dead give-away. "This is too much, Jean-Luc."

And when I lifted the lid, it became way too much. The black sequined clutch made my hand-me-down bag from Nina look like a 10p lunch bag from Woolworths.

"It's a two part gift, actually." There was trepidation in his voice, as if he didn't want to tell me more. "Melinda was at the boutique when I was there. She offered to tailor a dress for you – maybe something special to wear to the Copper Grove."

I could hardly breathe through the excitement, which made thinking straight almost impossible. Did he know her? He must've known her. Melinda Lazar didn't tailor dresses for girls like me. Her designs were reserved for supermodels, royalty and pop stars.

"How did you swing that, Jean-Luc?" I choked. "Tell me."

I didn't realise that I was gripping his arm until he moved. I let go in an instant.

"I've known her since I was a child." He grimaced as he spoke. "She was married to my father for a while. Needless to say, it didn't work out."

I tried not to appear too shocked by the revelation because this was classic Jean-Luc. He never volunteered information unless it was relevant to this situation at hand. I'd made no secret of my Melinda Lazar crush, but he saw no reason to mention their connection until he had no choice. It was maddening, but I'd come to accept that that was who he was – private to the point of cagy.

"That's shady behaviour, Jean-Luc," I scolded. "You could've told me earlier."

He stepped forward, taking my face in his hands. "I'm not the least bit close to her. That's probably why she hasn't rated a mention before now."

I couldn't be mad for a few reasons. First, he was kissing me. It was disarming, distracting and dead flippin' lovely. Second, he'd teed up dinner at the Copper Grove and a Melinda Lazar dress to go with it.

I had absolutely nothing to whine about – right up until I heard a key turn in the lock of the front door.

I was hoping it was Dmitry, but when I glanced at the clock on the wall and saw that it was five o'clock, I knew it would be Gordon. Our friendship had cooled since he took it upon himself to have a secret-spilling heart to heart with Jean-Luc. He meant well but I couldn't help feeling betrayed by it.

Gordon swanned into the kitchen wearing his usual stiff brown plaid accountant's suit, but he was also wearing a bright yellow feather boa, which was a tad confusing.

Clearly I wasn't the only one struggling. Jean-Luc squinted as if he was having trouble focusing. "Riri?" he teased. "Is that you?"

Gordon guffawed. "On sale at Fenwick." He flapped the end of the boa at him. "I couldn't resist."

The lull in conversation that followed was unpleasant, and Gordon must've felt the same way. He handed Jean-Luc a stack of mail and retreated to his room.

"Anything for me?" I asked hopefully.

He thumbed through the letters until he came across a pink envelope. I didn't even have to read it to know who it was from. Charlene was the only person I knew who drenched her letters in Jovan Musk before sending them.

Excitement got the better of me and I snatched it from him as he held it out. Jean-Luc didn't seem to notice. His eyes were transfixed on an official looking envelope that he'd shuffled to the top of the pile.

"Everything alright?" I asked.

"Fine," he replied, wandering out of the room.

I knew that was all the information he was going to give me so I didn't push for more. Figuring he could do with a minute alone, I sat at the kitchen table and read Charlene's letter. She prattled about everything and everyone, bringing me up to speed on all the goings-on at home.

Sharon got chucked out of the Gloucester Arms for pool sharking. She conned Trevor out of five quid and he complained to the manager.

Sharon's gunning for him now and Trevor's too scared to ride the busses in case she's waiting for him.

I laughed until my sides hurt, and then I almost cried. I missed my friends and I missed my mam, but I still felt like I was in the right place.

I was falling in love, gaining independence and I was broadening my horizons. None of those things are possible when you live in a place where backseat brawls on the bus are the highlight of your week.

CHAPTER 16

JEAN-LUC

WITH FIONA'S HELP, I'D BEEN ABLE TO STAVE OFF THE LETTER in my hand for over two months, but all the late nights she'd spent rewriting my essays had ultimately been for nothing. Despite the recent spike in grades, it wasn't enough to give me a passing grade for the semester.

I'd failed.

The feeling of having my whole future ripped from under me was so severe that I had to sit down. I slumped down on the edge of the bed and spent the next few minutes trying to figure out what the hell I was going to do with the rest of my existence.

It was a miserable turn of events that I was determined to keep to myself, so when Fiona walked into the bedroom, I tucked the letter into my back pocket and greeted her with the warmest smile I could muster.

She sat down beside me on the bed. "I got mail from Charl," she said, waving it at me. "She's a mad cow but I miss her."

I welcomed the light conversation, but my mind was too jumbled to continue it. I nodded, but stayed silent.

Fiona shifted, angling her body toward me as her hand moved to my cheek. "Please tell me what's going on." Her quiet voice was laced with concern. "What was that letter about?"

"It's just junk mail." I shrugged. "Something about discount encyclopaedias."

Lying didn't feel good but telling her the truth would've felt worse.

She dropped her hand to her lap. "I don't believe you," she mumbled. "You're shady as heck."

My smile was real this time. She called me out like no one else, and I loved it.

"You're the only thing in my life that makes sense, Fi," I said, reaching for her hand. "But I'm going to figure the rest out."

Fiona frowned, looking utterly confused. "A problem shared is a problem halved, Jean-Luc."

I couldn't begin to understand why I'd been gifted this girl. Fiona had shown me nothing but patience and under-standing since the first day we met, and all I'd done in return was keep her at arm's length. The thought of admitting that I was anything less than bulletproof was excruciating, but despite my thumping heart, I took the letter of doom from my pocket and handed it to her.

Fiona took forever to read it, slowly skimming her finger over every word.

I couldn't take it anymore. I rested my elbows on my knees and buried my face in my hands while I awaited her verdict.

Finally, she screwed up the letter and tossed it across the room. "I'm so sorry, Jean-Luc." She put her hand on my back. "I know how hard you worked. They obviously do too if they're offering to let you repeat the year."

"I'm not going to repeat, Fi," I muttered.

I felt her straighten up beside me as she pulled her hand away. "So that's it then? You're just going to give up?"

I turned my head to look at her. "I failed."

And I had a breakup letter from King's to prove it.

After a quick moment of thinking things through, she slapped her hands down on her knees. "Fine," she snapped. "Take a minute to wallow and be miserable."

"Then what?" I asked, cluelessly seeking instruction.

"You pick yourself up by the bootstraps and figure out your next move. That's how life works."

Considering the gravity of the situation, it was a lightweight suggestion. My whole future had been shot to pieces and she expected me to forge ahead as if it was repairable. "I can't expect you to understand th –"

"I understand everything." She angrily cut me off. "You feel like the rug has been pulled from under you. You feel hopeless and stupid and humiliated. Am I right?"

"Something like that, yes."

"I felt the same way when my dumb wedding plans turned to custard," she growled. "I got mad, took my revenge with a frozen chicken and moved onto better things - so don't tell me that I don't understand."

I reached for her hand to calm her down, but she quickly snatched it away.

"Maybe King's isn't the right fit for you," she continued. "But it doesn't mean the dream is dead."

"But what if it is?" I looked her straight in the eye. "What will happen to us?"

I wasn't sure what I was asking, but as usual, Fiona was way ahead of me. "You listen to me, Jean-Luc Décarie." She stood up, towering over me as if that was necessary to get her point across. "I don't care if you're a lawyer or a dustman. Rich or poor – I don't care. I love you without limitations. Why can't you accept that?"

I was a hateful, jaded person, that's why.

Questioning her motives was cruel and uncalled-for, and worst of all, it made her cry. I jumped to my feet and pulled her into my arms, desperate to repair the damage.

"I'm sorry," I whispered, over and over.

I'd spent my whole life surrounded by people who were constantly out to get something, in a world where image, credentials and pedigree meant everything. It was cutthroat, disingenuous and ruthless – and I'd been fighting to rise above it for far too long.

Fiona wasn't trying smash her way into that world. She was quietly and respectfully knocking on the door, without ever having a clue what was on the other side. I didn't want that life for her, but it was finally beginning to dawn on me that I didn't want it for myself either.

I took her face in my hands, inching her head back as I brushed tears from her cheeks with my thumbs. "*Vivre d'amour et d'eau fraîche*," I whispered.

"You can't stun me with pretty words any more, Jean-Luc," she sniffled. "I'm immune to your charms from now on."

"I know," I quietly replied. "But I'm going to work on changing that."

"How?"

I leaned in and kissed her for all I was worth, which happened to be millions upon millions of pounds. "Stay tuned, *Mademoiselle*," I murmured against her lips. "All will be revealed."

DIARY OF FIONA BLACK

WEDNESDAY, SEPTEMBER 14, 1983

According to Learn French In Ten Easy Steps, 'Vivre d'amour et d'eau fraîche' literally means to live on love and fresh water.
I have to learn this flippin language properly and stop relying on literal translations.
When Jean-Luc explained the actual meaning, it made a little more sense: Love is all you need.
I'm not sure if I believe it or not, but I like that he said it.
Book Of The Week: Capturing His Heart.
Adventure Fund: £100.12

CHAPTER 17

FIONA

WITH THE MELINDA LAZAR MEETING LOOMING OVER MY HEAD, anxiety was at an all time high. No matter how many times Jean-Luc assured me that I had nothing to worry about, I couldn't shake the feeling that I was going to make an idiot of myself.

"The only thing she's got on you is about thirty years and a few botched facelifts," he said, shoving a stack of papers into his book bag. "Remember that, okay?"

"Will you come with me?" I asked, nervously bouncing on the edge of the bed.

I already knew the answer; he was half-way to the door. "I can't, Fi." He looked at his watch. "I have a few things I need to take care of today and then I'm all yours."

"For how long?" I asked curiously.

He leaned down and kissed me as he passed. "For the rest of my days."

Jean-Luc turned back when he got to the door, flashing me a roguish smile that I didn't often see. Something had shifted. I wasn't sure what it was, but I knew it was important.

The French boy who made me giddy was still ridiculously handsome and debonair, but the invisible tension that kept him tightly wound and constantly stressed was gone.

"Getting kicked out of school looks good on you, Jean-Luc." I grinned. "You should do it more often."

He stalked back toward me, pushing me back on the bed as he covered my body with his. "There are many things I should do more often."

I watched as his gaze darted between my eyes and my mouth. "Are you trying to decide your next move, Napoleon?" I whispered.

"Yes, as it happens." My breath hitched in my throat as his warm lips touched my neck. "Bewitchery?" he murmured against my skin. "Or seduction?"

Jean-Luc's dark eyes never left mine as he slowly trailed his hand up my leg. I stayed silent and still, even when he slipped under my skirt.

"Choose your poison, Fi," he dared, hooking his thumb through the waistband of my tights. "Seduction or bewitchery?"

"Neither of those options are poisons," called a distant voice from the other side of the door. "Offer her cyanide – or a dose of hemlock, perhaps."

Nothing extinguishes molten lava quicker than Dmitry and his scientific ramblings. Jean-Luc moved, letting out a frustrated groan as he rolled onto his back.

"Socrates was condemned to death for impiety in 399BC," Dmitry continued. "A concentrated dose of hemlock is what did him in."

"We have to get out of this flat," I muttered. "Otherwise I'm going to die a virgin."

Jean-Luc brought my hand to his mouth and kissed my fingers. "I'm working on it."

"Getting us out of the flat or taking my virginity?" I asked.

"Both," he replied, smiling up at the ceiling. "In no particular order."

CHAPTER 18

JEAN-LUC

THE LAST TIME I SAW MY FATHER WAS AT A POLICE STATION AT three in the morning. He'd been arrested at a nightclub after he was found to be in possession of a small amount of cocaine.

I was furious that he'd called me, and even more furious with myself for going down there and bailing him out. Thierry acted like it was no big deal, and as it turned out, it wasn't. His overpaid team of lawyers managed to get the charges dismissed and he was back in the clubs a few nights later.

I couldn't stand being around him, which meant I was in for a bad day.

Holding my father's attention for longer than five minutes at a time was challenging so I figured the best place to meet him was somewhere he'd feel comfortable. I chose a pub near his home, and then called him to tee up a meeting there that afternoon.

"*Magnifique,*" he drawled. "I love to spend time with my boy."

"It's not a social get-together, Dad," I clarified.

There are consequences when you live your entire life being an irresponsible, reckless jerk. One of them is that your children eventually give up wanting to spend time with you. As thick-headed as Thierry was, he realised it.

He dropped the fatherly act in an instant. "I shall bring my cheque book then," he said sarcastically. "And wear my best clothes."

"No need," I replied. "Just bring your attorney. I've already met with mine."

~

I ARRIVED AT THE PUB HALF AN HOUR EARLY. MY FATHER WAS already there, sitting at the booth closest to the bar with a drink in his hand.

As expected, there was no greeting. "They call this rubbish cognac," he said, holding his glass up to the light. "It's an outrage."

"Send it back then," I suggested, sliding along the seat opposite him.

Thierry clicked his fingers, rudely beckoning the girl at the bar. "Come here, my darling," he demanded.

Not only did she comply, she practically ran across the room as if he was reeling her in by an invisible string.

"What is your name, my love?" he asked.

"Emma-Jayne," she replied.

My father leaned back in his seat, keeping a lock on her eyes as he continued the sugar-laced charm offensive. "Two names?" he asked. "How exotic and mysterious."

I couldn't help the sarcastic groan that escaped me as I slinked back in my seat. It probably had something to do with my exotic mysteriousness.

Clearly, Emma-Jayne was far more enamoured with his crap than I was. Her cheeks flushed red as she shifted her weight from foot to foot. "It's not that fancy," she said. "Me mum just called me after me two nannas."

If Thierry was thrown by her thick cockney accent, he didn't let on. He picked up his glass and held it out to her. "This, my darling, is an abomination," he told her. "I want you to take it away and bring me some absinthe. Do you know how to serve absinthe?"

She shrugged. "In a tall glass with ice?"

Thierry slowly shook his head, murdering her with a smouldering look that made him look damaged. "No, my love," he said pityingly. "I want you to go away and find a pontarlier glass, a cube of sugar, some iced water and an absinthe spoon. If you can do that, we'll move on."

She was frantically nodding before he'd even finished speaking, and when she turned to walk away, he slapped her on the behind.

I wanted her to be incensed and revolted, but she wasn't. I also wanted her to turn around and punch him in the mouth, but that didn't happen either. Instead, the giddy girl headed back to the bar to fulfil his obnoxious shopping list.

Dad turned his attention back to me. "Your old man has still got it, Jean-Luc."

I imagine he had a lot of things, most of which could be treated with ointment or psychotherapy, but he wouldn't have appreciated hearing it.

"Can we just move this along, please?" I asked, reaching for my book bag.

"Move what along?"

I tentatively slid the stack of paperwork across the table. "I want you to sign these," I said in French. "It's the release papers for my trust fund."

A huge grin swept his face. "*Enfin!*" he beamed.

I wasn't surprised by his reaction. I'd been eligible to claim my inheritance since the day I turned eighteen, but other than a small monthly allowance, it had remained largely untouched for the past five years. It was a decision that my father had never understood, and I'd never tried to explain it.

My family had wealth beyond measure, and no one in the past hundred years had lifted a finger to earn a penny of it. My plan had been to gain an education, make something of myself and work for a living. In my mind, that was the only way I could possibly justify being blessed with such a fortune.

I handed my father a pen. "I just need you to sign off on it."

"Why now?" He narrowed his eyes with suspicion. "What has changed your mind?"

"I want to tie up loose ends and go back to Marseille," I replied with a shrug. "It's where I belong."

"You wanted to study here." He drummed his forefinger on the table with every word spoken. "What has changed your mind?"

I wasn't used to him showing interest or parental concern. It was confusing, which might explain why I let my guard down and answered him. "I'm failing," I confessed. "I have to repeat the year or call it quits."

"Imbeciles!" He slammed his fist on the table. "Both of my sons are bright academics."

But only one of them was capable of getting an English law degree. My brother, Richard, had sailed through his studies. He still lived large on his inheritance, but no one ever questioned where his fortune came from because he worked at one of the most prestigious law firms in London.

"Calm down," I muttered.

"I will not," he shot back. "Who do I need to speak to? I will pay to keep you there."

"It doesn't work that way, Dad." I edged the papers nearer. "Just sign these and I'll go home and – "

"And live the life of a Décarie king," he interrupted. "It is your birthright, Jean-Luc; wine, women and song for the rest of your glorious days."

I stared across the table, trying to make sense of my father's ridiculous sense of entitlement. At best, his take on the world was adolescent. At worst, it was pathetic.

I saw no need to enlighten him that it was a lack of syntax skills that had derailed my studies. There was nothing wrong with my comprehension of the course work, and no reason why I couldn't pick up my studies in Marseille and excel.

Despite what he thought, I wasn't giving up, I was merely changing tack. But he was too focused on dragging me to the dark side to see it.

"And your woman? Are you taking her to France with you?" he asked.

"What woman?"

He leaned across the table and lowered his voice. "Melinda informed me that you have a girlfriend. I want to meet her."

I wasn't shocked that he knew about Fiona, or his outrageous demand to meet her. I would've been more surprised if Melinda hadn't given him the rundown after our impromptu meeting at the boutique.

"No," I replied, emphatically shaking my head. "She's just a passing fancy – no one important."

I felt the lie twisting in my gut but I managed to keep my expression even. The less my father knew about my relationship with Fiona, the better. It lessened the chances of him damaging it.

"That's the spirit," he praised. "It's much cheaper to retain the services of a pretty woman than a divorce lawyer."

Revulsion was starting to set in, which meant I'd reached

my limit. "Speaking of lawyers," I began, "yours was supposed to be here to look over the paperwork and witness your signature. Is he coming?"

"No."

"Why not?"

"Because I didn't ask him to." He picked up the papers and flicked through the pages. "Release of funds, blah, blah. Ownership of property, blah, blah." He laid the stack down on the table in a messy heap. "It's all there. Where do I sign?"

I didn't get a chance to reply. Emma-Jayne chose that moment to return to the table and impress Thierry with her foraging skills.

"Ta-daa," she sang, producing a pontarlier glass from behind her back. "I thought these were ice-cream glasses."

Thierry's ensuing laugh bordered on derisive, but Emma-Jayne didn't seem to notice. She dumped the rest of his requested items down on the table and ran back to the bar for a bottle of absinthe.

When she returned, he reverted to his idiotic Casanova impression. "Sit with me, darling," he purred, unscrewing the lid.

Emma-Jayne took a quick glance around the room before eagerly sliding into the booth beside him.

"This is how the French drink absinthe," he explained, pouring a shot of liquor into the glass. "And I want you to remember it for the rest of your life."

Thierry Décarie possessed a certain element of *je ne sais quoi* that made seemingly smart women behave like putty in his hands. It's not an affliction that lasts very long, but the effects can be harmful.

The smitten barmaid let out a squeaky giggle that made me roll my eyes. There was so much syrup in his voice that my feet should've been sticking to the floor.

My father laid the spoon across the glass and balanced the sugar cube on top.

Her eyes widened as if she was about to witness an act of sorcery. "That is amazing," she drawled.

"It's a lump of sugar," I said sarcastically. "Have you not seen one before?"

"Silence." He pointed at me but his eyes were fixed firmly on the glass. "Prepare to be astounded."

Seeing him dissolve the sugar by slowly dripping iced water over it wasn't the astounding part. It was Emma-Jayne's willingness to buy into his nonsense that blew my mind. The attractive young blonde with a killer smile should've considered herself to be miles out of his league, but she was hanging on his every word and Thierry knew it.

"I have given you one of my country's most cherished secrets." His eyes never left hers as he stirred the green drink. "You must tell no one."

I wanted to throw up. Every barmaid worth her salt knew how to properly serve absinthe, but she reacted as if he'd just committed treason against France. "I won't tell a soul," she promised, hand on heart.

"Good girl." Abandoning the roué act in an instant, he moved the glass out of the way and reached for the paper-work. After signing his name, he shoved it in her direction and pointed at the blank signature line. "Be a love and sign this for me."

Emma-Jayne didn't even question it. She scrawled her name, and then grabbed a napkin. "I want to give you my number," she said, already jotting it down.

I probably should've warned her against it, but didn't.

She rose to her feet and held out the napkin. "Maybe you can call me some time," she said hopefully.

My father snatched it from her grasp and stuffed it into his shirt pocket. "Don't hold your breath waiting, darling."

Emma-Jayne's smile slipped as she grabbed the bottle of absinthe and headed back to the bar, but Thierry wasn't the least bit affected by the humiliation he'd inflicted.

"Why would you do that?" I asked, appalled.

My father took a long sip of his drink before replying. "Because I can," he coolly replied. "It's a skill that separates me from the ordinary."

As far as I was concerned, it was a skill that separated him from humanity. My father perpetually treated people like dirt, and if that's what it meant to be a Décarie king, I wanted no part of it.

CHAPTER 19

FIONA

HEADING STRAIGHT TO THE BOUTIQUE FROM WORK SEEMED like a mistake. Not only was I incredibly nervous, I was sure I smelled like popcorn. I got off the bus early and walked the last few blocks in the hopes of airing my clothes, but it didn't slow me down.

I arrived half an hour early, much to the annoyance of the sales clerk. "You're early," she snapped, looking me up and down. "I don't know whether to praise you for your enthusiasm or mock you for it."

Her rudeness forced an apology from me that didn't seem right. Was there such a thing as being too punctual? Perhaps I'd broken one of the many rules of etiquette that I didn't understand.

"I can wait outside if you prefer," I offered.

"No need." She pointed to a small seating area near the changing room. "You can sit over there."

I wondered how Melinda would feel knowing that her sales assistant was an ill-mannered cow, but when I glanced around I realised that she couldn't have been too bad for business.

The whole joint screamed opulence and class, and every detail complemented the next. I loved the silver and pink colour scheme, particularly the pink crystals on the chandeliers. The only thing I didn't like was the bitch standing behind the counter.

"I'd be happy to wait," I said insincerely.

My heels sounded like a hammer smashing on the tiles as I made my way across the shop floor, but I didn't regret wearing them. Besides my new clutch, they were the most expensive accessory I owned and I felt elegant when I wore them. Unfortunately, the rest of my lady-like act was a sham, and the sales assistant knew it.

As soon as I sat down on the small Aztec print sofa, she pounced as if her main objective for the day was to make me feel as insignificant as dirt.

"Not from around here, are you?" she asked, cocking her head to the side.

"No," I confirmed, gripping my bag on my lap with two hands.

"I can tell." Her smirk made my skin prick. "No one would willingly take on that accent – or those clothes."

If Gill had been there she would've told the nasty mare to sod off, but I wasn't that courageous. My approach was to sit in silence and let her rip me to pieces.

"Your dress looks like an ill-fitting shirt held together with a belt," she taunted. "You should consider yourself lucky that Melinda's even prepared to look at you."

I wasn't feeling overly lucky at that point.

I didn't reply to her snarky comment, or the ten that followed. I sat in silence, looking anywhere but at her while I waited for Melinda to show up.

Eventually, she gave up and resumed thumbing through the magazine in front of her. I watched her for a while, trying to get my head around her appalling attitude, and that's when anger began to creep in.

From what I could tell, she had no reason to claim superiority. She was a sales girl in a boutique for crying out loud. The address was a little fancier than most, and the price tags had a few more numbers on them than I was used to, but she was still a sales girl.

I glanced at my watch. It was ten past four. "Do you think Melinda will be here soon?" I asked.

Her severe black bob didn't move an inch as she shook her head. "Why? Do you have somewhere else to be?" Her sour tone implied that she already knew the answer, but I replied anyway.

"No." I squared my shoulders. "I just assumed that she'd be here by now."

Ignoring my comment, the woman picked up the phone and used a pen to dial the number. I turned my attention to the window, trying not to make it obvious that I was eavesdropping.

"It's Melinda, darling," she murmured into the phone. "My four o'clock appointment is here. I thought you'd like to know."

I'd been plagued by many emotions that day, but now there was a new one in play – dazed confusion.

Who was she calling? And more importantly, if she was Melinda Lazar, why did she refer to herself in the third person?

It was weird. *She* was flippin' weird.

After hanging up the phone, the weirdo tossed her magazine aside and slowly stalked toward me. "Perhaps I should introduce myself," she said, extending her hand. "I'm Melinda Lazar, designer."

I expected her handshake to burn like acid, but it didn't. "Fiona Black," I muttered. "Why didn't you introduce yourself half an hour ago?"

She threw her head back and laughed – and her hair still didn't move. "I move at my own pace, darling," she replied pulling me to my feet. "Now, let me get a look at you."

Straight off the bat, I knew she was scrutinising more than my body shape, but I stood tall and held my head high as if I wasn't intimidated in the slightest.

"You're not what I was expecting," she commented. "I assumed Jean-Luc would prefer his diamonds to be a little more polished, but you have a nice figure so you're not a complete loss."

She probably expected me to bow at her feet and thank her for showing me mercy, but I was doing all I could not to smack her in the mouth. I swallowed away the humiliation and nodded.

Melinda moved to a nearby rack and began raking through the dresses. "I don't have the time or the inclination to start from scratch," she said. "I'll choose something off the rack for you. Something's bound to look decent."

I felt relieved by her lack of interest, which was an unexpected shift. I'd left the flat that morning with high hopes that she'd like me, but I hadn't put any thought into how I'd feel if I didn't like her.

"Try this." She thrust a sequined black gown at me. "You can change over there."

I barely even looked at the dress as I hung it on the hook in the changing room. I swiped the privacy curtain closed and focused on my reflection in the mirror.

Riri's voice filled my head, reminding me that no one had to right to make me feel inferior. There was nothing fabulous or posh about Melinda Lazar. She was little more than an acid tongued viper in stiletto heels. If that's what it took to be part of the upper crust, I was happy to stay put.

And I did…. for twenty-five minutes.

"Almost done in there?" Melinda impatiently called. "Or do you need me to dress you too?"

"I'm fine," I shot back. "I'll be out in a minute."

The snarky comeback I was expecting didn't come. She was distracted by someone entering the shop, and it took less than two seconds of spying through the crack in the curtain to find out who it was.

"Thierry!" Melinda beamed, rushing at him with open arms.

Years of reading romance novels had given me great insight when it came to visualising playboy lotharios, and if I had to build one from scratch, he would've looked just like Thierry Décarie.

His open neck shirt, collar length hair and tight jeans was in stark contrast to his son's clean-cut ways, but I couldn't deny that there was something about Thierry that made me take a second glance. The hard living lifestyle I'd heard so much about hadn't put a dent in his looks. He was dead gorgeous – in an old guy rock star kind of way.

"Why are you acting surprised to see me, Melinda?" He pushed his sunglasses to the top of his head. "You called me."

"Because you wanted to check out Jean-Luc's little tart," she hissed. "And don't pretend otherwise."

Thierry turned, staring so intently in my direction that I worried he could see through the thin curtain. I stood completely still, willing the ground to open and swallow me.

"I'm curious," he said, still staring. "He claims she is unimportant, but my son is a terrible liar."

Melinda let out an ugly cackle. "She's a northerner," she scoffed. "Trust me, she's unimportant."

It was impossible to believe that she thought I couldn't hear the conversation. Every nasty comment she'd made had been designed to cut me, and this was no different.

It was time to decide. I could either play dumb and

walk out there as if nothing was out of the ordinary, or I could try and scrape together some semblance of control and let them know exactly what northerner girls are made of.

A moment later, Thierry made the decision for me. "Come out, come out, wherever you are," he sang.

I truly was trapped in a nightmare, and it was starting to piss me off. I was there for a dress, not a character assassination – and if I was being honest, the dress wasn't looking that hot. I grabbed the hem and fanned it out, trying to breathe some life into it, but it was hopeless. The gown hung lifelessly, weighted down by big shoulder pads and sequins the size of pennies. It was ostentatious, excessive and far better suited to a woman triple my age who wore support stockings and sensible shoes.

Maybe she was trying to insult me.

"Who am I kidding?" I whispered to myself.

Of course she was trying to insult me. She'd been taking pot-shots at me since the minute I walked in. Dressing me in an ugly, inappropriate gown was her way of taking silent aim, and it was time to fight back.

Without giving any thought to the damage I might do to it, I ripped the dress off the hanger and bundled it up in my arms. "This is all wrong," I snapped. "I wanted an evening dress, not a sequined flour sack."

I threw open the curtain, bracing for the fallout as I alternated glances between them. Melinda's spiteful glare was in stark contrast to Thierry's expression. She looked like she wanted to do me in, but he just looked bewildered.

"You ungrateful little swine," she hissed through gritted teeth. "Who the hell do you think you are?"

"It doesn't matter who I am," I retorted. "What matters is that your dress is rubbish and I wouldn't be seen dead in it."

However futile it might've been, it felt good to return fire.

Thierry turned to Melinda and shrugged. "Better luck next time, my darling."

The string of expletives that tumbled from her mouth were better suited to the Gloucester Arms on a Saturday night than an upmarket King's Road boutique, but the effing and blinding got her nowhere. I refused to react, and Thierry's attention was elsewhere.

He folded his arms and rocked back on his heels, unashamedly looking me up and down. "Well, hello there."

His smooth accent was very familiar to me. The sleazy undertone was not.

"Hello." I nodded sharply in his direction, which was all the encouragement he needed to take a few steps closer.

"I am Thierry Décarie," he said, reaching for my hand. "Jean-Luc's father. And who might you be?"

I tried not to flinch when he kissed the back of my hand. "Fiona Black," I replied. "Jean-Luc's northerner tart."

Thierry turned, directing his scornful laugh at Melinda. "She has fire in her soul," he said. "I like her."

"That makes one of us," she spat.

There was no possible way that the conversation could recover. I needed to shut it down and get the hell out of there, but Thierry wasn't finished with me.

"How long have you known my son?" he asked.

I shrugged. "A while."

He narrowed his eyes. "You think you've struck gold with him, don't you?"

I refused to answer because it felt like a trap. I *had* struck gold, but not in the way he was implying.

"You haven't, my love," he continued, sticking his bottom lip out and pouting like a child. "Jean-Luc has no intention of taking you back to Marseille with him."

"He's leaving?" asked Melinda. "Why?"

I was glad she butted in. It saved me from looking foolish by asking the same question.

"He failed his studies," he said. "They kicked him out of school."

Thierry's flippant tone implied that it was no big deal. He had no idea how hard Jean-Luc had worked to keep his head above water, or how devastating it was not to scrape a passing grade. But he did know that he'd flunked, and considering they were barely on speaking terms, that was far more information than he should've been privy to.

My mind was spinning with so many thoughts that I struggled to focus on any of them. I knew nothing about Jean-Luc's plans of skipping the country, but it was important not to feel hurt by the revelation.

Jean-Luc was cagy and evasive because I allowed him to be, but he wasn't a liar and he wasn't a cad, which is more than I could say for Thierry.

The whole conversation felt like an act of vandalism. Melinda had been bashing away at me for no other reason than she could. Thierry's motives weren't yet clear, so I stood back and let him take another jab.

"Perhaps you distracted him, Fiona." His lecherous eyes raked up and down my body. "Jean-Luc is usually such a focused young man."

Melinda sat down on the couch and let out a raucous laugh. "Focused on being an arsehole, you mean."

Thierry leaned closer. "It's true," he confirmed with a smirk. "He's a bit of a problem child."

"Damaged," she corrected. "He's damaged."

"Yes," agreed Thierry with a chuckle. "But his mother is dead and I have no patience. It's to be expected."

It was impossible to believe he was speaking so cold-heartedly about his own flesh and blood. I didn't care how many ladies-in-waiting he'd shagged, he was awful and I never wanted to see him again.

"I hope he does go back to Marseille." My voice was quiet but the lock I held on his eyes didn't waver. "The further he stays away from you, the better off he'll be."

Thierry barely reacted, but Melinda was incensed. She jumped to her feet and stalked toward me, only to be held back by her knight in rusty armour. "Leave her be," he warned. "She can't be held accountable for her ignorance. Look at her for Christ's sake – low-hanging fruit."

I look fine, I told myself.

I was also calm, unaffected and well and truly done with the House of Lazar and the cretins who hung out there.

"Here," I said, thrusting the bundled-up dress at Melinda. "Take this."

"Keep it," she sourly replied. "I'll never get the commoner stench out of it."

Perhaps impressed by her remark, Thierry slung his arm around her shoulder and kissed her cheek. I wondered what he was praising her for but fought back the urge to ask. Instead, I tucked the ugly dress under my arm, walked out of the store and never looked back.

❧

THERE COMES A TIME WHEN YOU HAVE TO CHOOSE BETWEEN turning the page and closing the book. I'd been there a hundred times, but never in real life.

Turning my back on fictional stories is easy. If I don't like the characters or can't relate to the plot, I toss it aside and move on.

Real life doesn't work that way, but if it did, I might've closed the book. I didn't like the characters and I wasn't even sure what the plot was.

I arrived back at the flat at a little after six with an over-whelming urge to binge on chocolate, take a two hour bath and soak the entire saga out of my head.

I just wanted to be left alone, but I didn't even make it to the door without interruption.

"Miss Black," called a voice from above. I looked up to see Lady Kitty standing on the third floor landing, flapping a piece of paper at me. "Will you be so kind as to pass this on to Mr Décarie?"

I shrugged. "What is it?"

"One does not bellow across the halls," she scolded.

Considering the day I'd had, snapping back at her would've been justified – but one does not snap at Lady Kitty.

I grabbed the railing and slowly trudged up the stairs as if my swish heels were made of lead. By the time I reached the landing, Kitty had retreated to her flat.

Seriously annoyed, I knocked on the door.

"Miss Black," she announced as the door swung open. "Do come in." As soon as I stepped inside, she handed me a tiny crystal glass. "An afternoon sherry," she explained with a smile.

I studied the way Lady Kitty held her glass and tried my best to mimic her. "What do you want me to give Jean-Luc?" I asked.

She handed me a piece of paper. "A receipt for the rent."

I glanced down at the handwritten note, trying to make sense of her elaborate scrawl. "But they only just paid it."

"He gave notice of his intention to vacate the premises and kindly paid three months of rent." Kitty sat down, motioning to the brown velvet armchair beside her. "Sit, darling," she instructed. "You look faint."

I slumped down in the chair, concentrating all my energy on not spilling my drink as the world began to crumble around me. Thierry was a jerk, but as it turns out, he was a truthful jerk. Jean-Luc *was* planning to do a runner.

"Are you going to stay in London?" she asked. "I presume the extra rent was to cover your portion. He strikes me as a very generous young man."

"Generous to a fault," I muttered. "With everything except his thoughts and feelings."

"He never told you he was leaving?"

"No." I set my glass down on the side table. "Jean-Luc doesn't tell me anything."

"Men are difficult creatures," she said pityingly. "My Ronald was impossible at times, but we were married for forty-three good years." Kitty pointed to a picture on the wall. "He worked as a freight conductor for the railways. It was a very important job."

I stood up and walked over to get a better look, mainly to hide my confusion. Since when do lords work jobs at the railways?

I squinted at the framed photo, taking in the small details that shouldn't have mattered, but did. Lord Ronald was just an average looking bloke, free of ponce and superiority. He wore a tweed newsboy cap, a kind smile and a coat that had seen better days.

Things weren't adding up. I turned around and covertly checked out the rest of the room. It was then that I noticed that decorating scheme was better suited to an eccentric hoarder than an aristocrat.

The display cabinets that lined every wall were over-flowing with china and crystal, but most pieces were odd and mismatched. The furniture wasn't grand and the flat was in the same state of ill repair as the rest of the building.

"Did you inherit your title, Lady DeVille?" I asked curiously.

Her demure laugh had an edge of wickedness that made

me smile. "I *invented* my title, darling," she replied. "I have devoted my lifetime to preserving the art of etiquette and good standing." She took a sip from her glass. "I *am* a lady, despite my circumstance."

"I want to be a lady too." The awkward admission hitched in my throat. "Until today, I thought it was all about money and class, but I was wrong."

"What changed your mind, darling?"

My eyes drifted to the designer gown poking out of the top of my bag. "I guess I woke up to the fact that not all rich people have class."

"Indeed," she said knowingly.

I let out an exaggerated sigh. "I'm just looking for a flippin' fairy-tale, Lady Kitty. Is that too much to ask for?"

"Good grief, girl. I suggest you stop looking." She huffed out a hard laugh. "Create your own fairy-tale and stop letting others dictate the story."

It might've been the most empowering advice I'd ever been given. Dining at five star restaurants while wearing sequined couture shouldn't have been a life goal for any self-respecting young woman. It wasn't a true measure of worth or success, and I felt embarrassed that I'd wasted so much time thinking otherwise.

"Where do I start?" I asked.

The most elegant and glamorous woman I had ever met wasted no time in doling out some sage advice. "Find your own identity, Miss Black." She put her hand to her heart. "She's in there somewhere."

I smiled. "Do you think she might be a lady?"

"Aim higher, darling," she encouraged. "She might just be a queen."

CHAPTER 20

JEAN-LUC

CHANGING THE ENTIRE COURSE OF MY LIFE IN A MATTER OF hours was supposed to feel liberating and brave, but I spent the whole day feeling like I'd swallowed a coil of barbed wire.

Throughout the ages, a million tales depicting idealistic stories of love, attainment and everything in between have been written. The problem I faced was that Fiona had read all of them, and I couldn't be sure if the life I could offer would measure up.

What if she didn't want to go to France? Or worse, what if she didn't want to go to France with me? Fiona already thought I was devious and vague. How would she take the news that I'd been making plans behind her back?

Thinking about it caused me physical damage. By the time I arrived home, my stomach was in knots and my brain was fried. It was as if I could hear her voice in my ear, demanding to know what I was up to. And then I realised I wasn't imagining it.

My eyes flitted in every direction until I finally spotted her, leaning over the balustrade on the third floor landing. "What are you up to?" she repeated.

To my relief, she didn't sound accusatory or angry, which meant it was likely a simple greeting that I didn't need to overthink.

"I just got home," I replied, smiling up at her. "How did your meeting with Melinda go?"

"It was fine." Her pretty face twisted as if she was fighting a scowl. "I got a dress. Do you want to see it?"

"Of course," I lied.

"Great," she beamed, throwing her arm wide. "Without further ado, allow me to introduce the fabulous, the beautiful, Lady Kitty DeVille."

Fiona embarked on a one-woman round of applause as Kitty swanned into view wearing a black dress. Clearly, the shopping expedition hadn't been fine. If the gown had already been rehomed, I could only assume that Fiona didn't like it.

London's most peculiar landlady was impressed, though. She sashayed and twirled as if she was parading before an audience of thousands. "Mr Décarie," she crowed. "How lovely of you to join us. Miss Black was fearful that you'd absconded without saying goodbye."

The applause stopped in an instant as Fiona whipped her head in Kitty's direction. "I never said that," she hissed.

Kitty ignored her. "I told her that you were much too noble for that kind of skulduggery."

Fiona looked outraged but it was neither the time nor place to reminded her that Kitty was prone to bending the truth. The best course of action was to play along. "Lady DeVille, I could never leave London without Fiona."

The meddlesome woman stood beside her as if Fiona needed the protection. "How is she to know that?" she asked. "You haven't breathed a word of your intentions."

"My intentions were supposed to be a surprise," I replied. "But you're making it difficult to follow through."

"A surprise?" asked Fiona. "I love surprises."

I smiled up at her. "You don't think it's suspect behaviour?"

"You tell us," interjected Kitty.

"It was a surprise intended for Fiona," I said, darting my eyes between the two of them. "But I'm prepared to share the basics."

The sequined dress rattled as Lady DeVille indulged in another twirl. "The floor is yours, young man."

She didn't mean it but I forged ahead anyway. "I was going to explain everything over dinner on Saturday."

Fiona's shoulders slumped. "You're leaving, aren't you?"

"I want to get my studies back on track, Fi," I explained. "Attending school in France is the only hope I've got now."

Fiona began a slow descent down the stairs. "You didn't have to go to the trouble of dinner," she said, stopping half way. "And I certainly don't need to be wearing a couture gown when you break the terrible news."

I was shaking my head before she'd even finished speaking. "You've got it all wrong," I told her. "I don't want to go anywhere without you."

"You're making no sense, Jean-Luc," she grumbled.

"He knows exactly what to say," said Kitty with a haughty giggle. "Until he has to actually say it."

My head snapped in Kitty's direction. "You're not helping, Lady DeVille."

Ignoring me completely, she turned to Fiona. "He wants you to go with him, darling," she assured her. "I suspect the fanfare of dinner was a prelude to a proposal of marriage."

Yet again, Kitty's big mouth had pushed the conversation in the wrong direction. I had no intention of proposing. Asking Fiona to give up her life in England and come to Marseille was fraught with enough danger without adding marriage to the mix.

Fiona's wide-eyed stare was directed at me, but her frustration was reserved for Kitty. "Don't put words in his mouth," she scolded. "I have enough trouble getting him to speak as it is."

"I shall say no more," she promised, flouncing toward her door. "I'm sure you're capable of sorting the wheat from the chaff."

When her door closed and she was safely contained behind it, I pulled in a long breath and sat down on the bottom step. When Fiona sat beside me, I asked an odd question. "Am I wheat or chaff?"

She bumped my arm with her shoulder. "Both probably have some nutritional value."

"Your mother once asked me if I was silk or cotton," I replied, putting my hand on her knee. "I can only assume comparison to inanimate objects is an English thing."

There wasn't much humour in her quiet laugh, but it was comforting to hear it. "Perhaps," she agreed.

"This day has not turned out how I planned, Fi."

"My expectations were far too high as well," she replied. "Did you see that horrible dress?"

"How could I not?" I asked. "Your model wore it loudly."

"Melinda chose it," she revealed, angling her body toward me. "I think it was meant as an insult."

It was too much to hope that my ex step-monster could rein herself in and play nicely. Giving her the benefit of the doubt was stupid, and I felt the immediate need to apologise for it.

"It's not your fault," Fiona insisted. "She's vile and your father is no prize either."

"Thierry was there too?" I sounded surprised but wasn't. Warning him to steer clear of her was akin to waving a red rag at a bull.

"Yes," she confirmed, "But I don't think I made a very good impression. He called me low-hanging fruit."

My head lolled forward. "Oh, my god," I muttered, burying my face in my hands. "How shameful can one man be?"

Fiona grabbed my forearm, prising my hand away. "I'm not upset, Jean-Luc, and I don't want you to be either," she said.

"I should have come with you."

Fiona hooked her arm through mine and shuffled closer. "You can't protect me from everything," she told me. "I love that you try, but if you keep it up you're going to give yourself a flippin' ulcer."

I had to concede that shielding her from the ugly parts of my life was tiresome. People like Thierry and Melinda were always going to slip through the cracks and wreak havoc, and there was nothing I could do to stop it.

"I'm more than willing to take the good with the bad," she added. "And I'm very capable of sorting the wheat from the chaff."

I didn't share her level of self-assurance, and I knew I never had. It drove home that fact that I needed this girl in my life, and her answer to my next question would determine whether the feeling was mutual.

I stood up, and dropped to one knee in front of her.

"Oh no," she protested, quickly pulling away when I reached for her hand. "Please don't do anything foolish, Jean-Luc."

It was then that I realised I'd set the scene wrong. I was down on one knee, probably sporting a terrified but hopeful expression. "I'm not going to propose," I assured her.

She let out a long sigh of relief. "Thank heavens for that," she said. "Neither of us are ready for that kind of caper."

I gave an uneasy smile as I rose to my feet. "I had some-thing a little more low-key in mind."

She reached for my hand, pulling me down beside her. "I'm listening."

Making eye contact with her was a mistake. Seeing her hopeful expression sapped the last bit of courage I had. As a result, the tangled mess of words that tumbled from my mouth came out sounding like a poorly planned business proposition. "I do want you to come to Marseille with me," I began. "The opportunities there are plentiful. You could continue learning French, or get a job if you want to – what-ever makes you happy."

I felt her crumple beside me. "Sounds like you've got it all worked out."

She was wrong. I had no clue what I was doing.

"Please, Fi." I held her hand tighter. "I need you."

"Because you're scared to make the leap on your own?"

"No, because I need you."

She frowned, obviously not the least bit enamoured. "You're not exactly selling this plan, Jean-Luc."

In an involuntary show of defeat, my shoulders sagged. "I know the words are all wrong but the sentiment is there," I mumbled.

Fiona shuffled closer to me. "I'll give you a chance to work on the delivery," she offered. "I'm not a complete sap, Jean-Luc, but I need a little bit of mush. You're asking me to run away to France with you. At least throw a bit of romance into it."

"I truly don't know how."

"Sure you do." She bumped my shoulder. "Fiona, my love," she crowed melodramatically. "I cannot spend a minute on this earth without you. Follow me to Marseille." She threw her hand out, accidentally slapping me in the process. "We shall eke out a living busking on the streets, returning to our modest log cabin at night to make love and revel in the splendour of our union."

My inheritance guaranteed that there would be no busking or log cabins for us, but I chose not to enlighten her because I didn't want to taint her decision.

"Is that the dream, Fi?" I grinned. "Log cabins and busking?"

"God no." She scrunched up her pretty face. "I still want castles and diamonds but we all have to start at the bottom."

My laugh was the sound of total relief. It occurred to me that she probably thought Thierry bankrolled my life. In truth, he hadn't given me a penny in years. The Décaries of generations past were the ones who looked after me, and I was going to do them proud by creating a good life packed with hard work and success. That was *my* dream, and if I had been capable of explaining it, I would've told Fiona that she was an integral part of it.

"Please say you'll come." The desperation in my tone didn't bother me. I *was* desperate. "You're the best thing that's ever happened to me."

Her smile was faint, but at least she smiled. "You're still a mystery to me, Jean-Luc."

"I'm beginning to realise that I'm a mystery to myself at times," I replied. "But I'm trying to live more in the moment and relax a little, which is why returning to Marseille appeals."

"We're both guilty of trying to control our destinies," she said quietly. "I've decided to abandon my social climbing efforts. I think it's dog-eat-dog world and I'm a clumsy puppy."

I leaned across and chastely kissed her cheek. "I happen to like puppies."

"Yeah, well, I happen to like shady French boys with broad shoulders and lovely smiles so I guess we're golden."

"So you'll come?" I asked hopefully.

After what seemed like an eternity of deliberation, she finally spoke. "The only thing I would lose by not going is you." Her dark blue eyes burned a hole through to my very soul. "And that would be a terrible waste of a fairy-tale ending."

DIARY OF FIONA BLACK

SATURDAY, SEPTEMBER 16, 1983

*Jean-Luc said the man on the phone nearly choked when he called
to cancel our reservation at the Copper Grove. Maybe it's never
been done before.*
I guess that makes us pioneers.
*In another first, I swallowed my pride and made up with Riri. I
couldn't bear the thought of leaving London without mending our
friendship.*
*I laid it all on the line and told her she was a knob for spilling my
secrets to Jean-Luc. She laughed, and said I was a knob for making
him eat cucumber sandwiches against his will.*
In the morning, we'll leave London town behind.
*It didn't take a lot of soul searching to realise it's a good move
for us.*
*English law is not for Jean-Luc, and English society is a nut I'll
never crack.*
Sod the dream!
Hopefully we'll carve our own path and make new ones.
<u>Book Of The Week</u>: Slighted Love.
<u>Adventure fund</u>: £97.30

CHAPTER 21

FIONA

IN THE NINETEENTH CENTURY, THERE LIVED A MAN CALLED Rainier Décarie who owned a very successful shipping company. He amassed a great fortune over the years, and used some of it to build a huge mansion on a cliff overlooking the Bay of Marseille. From there, he could keep a close eye on his fleet of ships as they sailed from port.

That bloke had long since passed, but the house remained in the family, passed down to the youngest son of each generation on the day he turns eighteen.

It was the kind of story that someone might tell over dinner – an interesting anecdote designed to impress – but I didn't hear it over dinner. I heard it on the cab ride from the airport, en route to said mansion.

"Why haven't you told me this before?" I asked.

Jean-Luc hesitated, glancing at me only briefly. "I didn't want to scare you away."

"Why would I be scared?"

He looked at me again, this time holding my gaze. "Because I am currently the youngest Décarie son," he said simply.

ON A SCALE OF GRANDEUR FROM ONE TO TEN, CHÂTEAU Rainier was off the charts. I thought Buckingham Palace was the finest building in existence, but I'm sure it has nothing on this joint.

Unbelievably, every square foot of it belonged to Jean-Luc, and as if that revelation wasn't hard enough to grasp, he topped it off with the news that he'd recently signed off on his trust fund.

"It's a substantial amount of money, Fi," he said sheepishly. "But I don't want it to change anything between us."

Too late.

Everything had changed. I'd been dreaming of a princess existence for as long as I could remember, but achieving it was supposed to be a process. I couldn't fathom how I'd cope with being thrown in at the deep end.

We stood for a long time, gazing up at the monstrous house at the top of the driveway. I had no idea what was running through Jean-Luc's mind, but mine was busy weighing up my options. I couldn't deny that the trappings of a privileged life was something I longed to have, but it didn't define me. Some things are more important than money – like honesty and truth.

I turned to Jean-Luc. "This isn't enough for me," I told him. "You have to give me more."

To most, it would've sounded greedy and arrogant, but he knew exactly what I meant. If we were going build a life together, he needed to drop his guard and speak.

"I'll tell you everything," he promised.

Garnering information from Jean-Luc was notoriously difficult so I wasn't expecting much, but for once, he had plenty to say.

When he turned eighteen, he inherited a huge amount of

money. Thanks to the savvy entrepreneurialism of ancestors like Rainier, it was a perk that every Décarie enjoyed – except Jean-Luc wasn't enjoying it at all.

"It's been sitting in trust ever since," he explained.

"For five years?" I asked. "Why have you left it so long?"

His line of sight drifted to the ground. "Because I'm not worthy of that kind of handout," he quietly replied. "I don't feel like I deserve it."

Most people would've taken the money and run, just like his father had. But Jean-Luc was nothing like Thierry. Above all else, he was righteous and good.

"Life shouldn't be a free ride, Fi," he added, lifting his head to look at me. "I want a successful career and a good education. I want to contribute to my family's legacy, not leech off it."

The French boy's armour was finally beginning to crack, shining light on pieces that only I could see. Contrary to the tough front he presented to the world, he was not a man who had it all together, and at twenty-three, that was how it was supposed to be.

I reached up and took his face in my hands. "You will," I assured him. "You can be whoever you want to be."

His eyes flitted from my eyes to my mouth. "So can you," he murmured.

I tilted his head, locking his gaze. "I'm not sure who I want to be yet."

"Me neither," he replied, dipping his head to kiss me. "But if you're willing, we'll figure it out together."

~

THE GRAND TOUR OF CHÂTEAU RAINIER BEGAN IN THE HUGE lounge room at the back of the house. It had gazillion dollar views of the bay, but it was the décor that held my attention.

Baroque in design, every stick of furniture was intricately carved, oversized and precious. The huge arched windows were framed by billowy sheer drapes, and oriental silk rugs covered the oak floor. It was opulent, grand, and like nothing I'd ever seen before – even in my dreams.

I walked along the length of the velvet sofa, absently running my fingertips along the top as I tried to take it all in. So far, I wasn't hooked. Château Rainier was feeling a little icy and stiff.

Jean-Luc must've read my mind. "Not all the rooms are this formal," he said.

I forced a smile that didn't feel genuine. "I can't imagine what growing up here would've been like, Jean-Luc."

"I have very fond memories of this place," he replied, moseying toward me. "When my mother was alive it was a wonderful home. I'm sure we can make it a homely again." His arms slipped around my waist. "We'll redecorate."

I inched my head back to look at him. "We can do that?"

"We can do whatever we please, *Mademoiselle*," he replied. "There are no rules."

"I have rules, Napoleon," I linked my arms around his neck and tried my hand at batting my eyelashes. "But I'm prepared to break a few for you."

I must've pulled off the temptress look with some degree of skill. Before I knew it, my feet left the ground and we were heading toward the stairs.

~

IN KEEPING WITH THE REST OF THE HOUSE, JEAN-LUC'S childhood bedroom was overloaded with antique furniture and expensive fixtures from a bygone era. It was a far cry from our shabby digs in London, and I loved it.

I took my time when it came to checking it out, even at

the risk of killing the giddy moment we were having. "I've never seen a four-poster bed before," I said, spinning back to face him. "It's dead romantic."

Jean-Luc folded his arms, casually leaning against the doorframe. "I've always hated that bed," he replied. "It's a terribly feminine piece for a boy's room, don't you think?"

"I adore it," I declared with a wistful sigh. "The only thing missing is a lace canopy."

Clearly uninterested in continuing a conversation about the décor, he worked to shut it down. "You can redecorate until your heart's content, *Mademoiselle*."

"My heart is already content, Jean-Luc," I said slowly stalking toward him. "My body, on the other hand, is feeling a little antsy."

CHAPTER 22

JEAN-LUC

MY ONE HOPE GOING FORWARD WAS THAT LOVE WOULD ALWAYS be louder than the pressure to be perfect. Something had altered, and I found myself looking at my future in an entirely different way. I was less one-track now, and more open to the idea of adjusting my course.

I was still committed to a career in law, but other dreams were creeping in, and at that moment, she was standing in front of me, pinning me in place with a gorgeous cerulean stare.

Being truly alone was a first for us, but Fiona had bigger firsts on her mind. More than anything, I wanted her to feel at ease but when she broke my gaze and wandered toward the window, I knew nerves were getting the better of her.

I followed, slipping my arms around her from behind. "Are you okay?" I whispered, resting my chin on her shoulder.

Rather than answer my question, she swept the curtains aside and made some generic comment about the view.

"Yes, it's wonderful," I agreed, murmuring the words against her neck.

Her grip on the curtain remained. "These curtains are silk," she noted, rolling the fabric between her fingers. "Do you know how expensive dupioni is?"

"No," I replied. "Tell me."

"My Mam charges ten quid a yard for it."

I had it on good authority that her extortion price was much higher, but I kept quiet. I had no desire to start a conversation about Nellie and her thuggish intimidation tactics. My focus was solely on her daughter.

Fiona twisted in my arms, pressing herself against me. The afternoon sun streaming through the window caught the side of her face, showcasing just how beautiful she was.

I wanted to mention the stunning colour of her eyes, but she'd heard it a million times before. I wanted to kiss her lips too, but even that seemed cliché at that point.

Fiona didn't utter a word as my hand settled on the knot securing her wraparound blouse. She still didn't speak as I gingerly untied it, but when her shirt fell open and I leaned in to kiss her, she unceremoniously put the brakes on.

"Wait, wait, wait," she whispered, holding me at arm's length with a hand on my chest. "I have to ask you something first."

Her desperate tone gave the impression that a life or death question was on its way, but I should've known better.

"Jean-Luc, what if we're incompatible as lovers?" she asked.

I felt perplexed and amused in equal measure, and shaking my head didn't shift it. "Fi, what are you talking about?"

I wasn't the least bit shocked when she pulled a tatty book out of the back pocket of her jeans. It was a move I'd seen a hundred times, and I decided long ago that publishers make trashy novelettes compact for this very reason – portability for quick reference.

Still a little breathless, she hurriedly thumbed through the book until she found the page she was looking for. "Disappointment struck Randolph's heart with the force of an anvil," she read out loud. "Bernice, the woman of his dreams, had turned out to be a lazy and unresponsive lover."

I slowly shook my head. "Was she dead, Fi?" I bowed my head, trying to hide my smile. "Maybe the poor woman was dead."

"No," she replied, turning her attention back to the book. "She was all over him on page twelve."

"Then perhaps he was a lousy lover," I suggested, wiggling my eyebrows. "Bernice might've been bored."

I didn't need to point out that she was being slightly neurotic. Within seconds, she figured it out herself. "I'm overthinking things, aren't I?" she asked.

Nothing good would come from answering her. Instead, I took a step forward, wrenched the book from her grasp and dropped it on the floor. "Have you seen *Gone With The Wind*?" I murmured the question against her lips.

I thought she shook her head, but it was hard to tell. Her entire body was trembling. "It's one of my favourite movies," I revealed, slowly sliding her blouse off her shoulders. "Much more insightful than The Adventures of Bernice and Rudolph."

"Randolph," she breathlessly corrected.

"Whatever." I tossed her shirt on a nearby chair. "In it, Rhett says to Scarlett, 'You should be kissed and often, and by someone who knows how'."

Her fingers tangled through my hair, holding me against her as I kissed a long line across her chest. "Maybe I'll read that book instead," she whispered.

"You do that, *Mademoiselle*." I pressed my smile against her skin. "But not today."

DIARY OF FIONA BLACK

SUNDAY, SEPTEMBER 17, 1983

Today I lost my virginity to the boy who loves me. It played out on
a four-poster bed in a mansion on the Mediterranean coast.
How's that for a flippin fairy-tale?
I was kissed, and often, by someone who definitely knew how.
Book Of The Week: Gone With The Wind
Adventure fund: Who cares?

The End

EPILOGUE

Jean-Luc

When two perfectionists fall madly in love, there's no such thing as going with the flow. Fiona and I had very definite ideas when it came to making a life together, and for a while, everything went to plan.

My focus was on my studies, and hard work was soon rewarded with strong grades. The struggle I endured at King's faded into distant memory and before long, a degree in law was back within my grasp.

Fiona quickly found her niche too. After learning French in record time, she moved to mastering the art of *savior faire*.

Three times a week, at six o'clock on the dot, an uppity tutor would turn up at our door. She brought with her an alligator skin bag, a puckered expression and ten million rules regarding etiquette.

I couldn't bear the drama of it, but Fiona soaked in every lesson as if knowing the difference between and cake fork and a fish fork was her main calling in life.

I'd never understood her fascination with pomp and

ceremony, but I couldn't deny it suited her. With knowledge comes confidence, and before long she was ready to strike out on her own and ditch her pucker-faced coach.

Her next venture came after a chance meeting at a café at the Old Port. I hadn't seen Jessica Décarie for a long time, but we picked up where we left off and spent hours catching up over lunch. Stepmother number three was in Marseille on business. When she mentioned she was looking for someone to assist with organising the Sunkiss Foundation's latest charity gala, I suggested that Fiona might be a good candidate.

Within an hour of meeting her, Jessica offered Fi the job, and just like that, she had a new calling.

Apart from cooking, Fiona excelled at everything she tried her hand at. I loved her drive and determination. In fact, I loved everything about her.

Every box was ticked. I didn't think life could be any more perfect, but then fate proved me wrong by sending us headlong down a road that wasn't even on our map.

Ryan was born just ten months after our move to Marseille. From the minute I laid eyes on him, I knew he'd forever be my greatest accomplishment, but for the first year or so, he was also my biggest struggle. I could've blamed it on my father and the poor example he'd set, but in truth, I was just clueless.

I was too frightened to hold him until someone showed me how, and his tiny cry would send a shiver of fear right through me. Fortunately for all of us, Fiona was a wonderful mother from the get-go. She was also mighty unforgiving when it came to dealing with my ineptitude. It was trial by fire, and she held my feet to the flames until I became the engaged, hands-on father that she knew I wanted to be.

I eventually found my stride, and in the blink of an eye,

our tiny baby morphed into a busy, curious toddler who seemed to believe he was indestructible.

Before long, the entire house was baby-proofed. We had gates blocking off the stairs, cable ties on cabinet doors, and a wonderfully energetic nanny who was two steps behind Ryan at all times.

Mrs Brown was a godsend. Getting through the day with one boisterous little boy in tow was one thing, but two was a game changer.

Three years after Ryan's birth, Adam arrived. He was as adorable as his brother, but that's where the similarities ended. Ryan was busy, rowdy and demanding, and had been since the day he was born. Adam was quiet, content and placid – and his mother was a nervous wreck because of it.

Not long after we brought him home, I arrived home from work to find Fiona keeping vigil in the nursery. She was sitting on the chair by the window, inches away from the bassinette. Even from the doorway, I could tell that she was weepy and tired.

"Long day, *Mademoiselle?*"

"Ryan took it upon himself to test out his new swearword on the postman," she listlessly replied.

I cringed, and then asked a very important question. "*Anglais ou français?*"

"French." She scowled at me. "This one's on you, superstar."

"I said it one time." My reply got caught in a laugh. "Clever little devil."

"He's both of those things."

I wandered over to the bassinette and peered down at the sleeping baby. "I'll talk to him," I promised.

"I already did." Her shaky voice threatened tears at any moment. "I told him if he does it again I'll wash his mouth out with soap."

I turned back to face her. "Did it work?"

"No," she grumbled. "The little sod took it upon himself to venture off to the bathroom and give the soap a lick. My guess is he's weighing up his options."

Laughing did not end well for me. Fiona burst into tears.

Completely at a loss, I crouched down in front of her. "What's the matter?" I asked, tucking her hair behind her ear. "Talk to me."

"I came across a very worrying magazine article today," she sniffled. "It was about genetic predisposition."

My interest in the upcoming conversation was nil. As far as I was concerned, the tacky magazines she favoured were as dangerous as her trashy romance novels.

"It said that dimples are a genetic defect caused by short-ened facial muscles," she continued.

I frowned, unable to make sense of her rising panic "So?"

"So, Adam has a dimple in his cheek."

We'd noticed it the second we laid eyes on him. It was so obvious that even Ryan saw it, and then demanded to know who had poked a hole in his brother.

When I left for work that morning it was a cute and unique trait. One piece of shoddy journalism and eight hours later, it was a defect.

"Be reasonable, Fi," I pleaded, reaching for her hand.

She pulled away. "We should get it checked out," she insisted. "The magazine said it's a deformity."

I stood up and leaned into the bassinette, studying my adorable newborn son. "You're right, my love," I said dryly. "He's an abomination."

"You're not taking me seriously," she grumbled.

I refused to take her seriously, but telling her so was going to take an enormous amount of tact. I stepped away from the baby and pulled her to her feet. Taking her face in my hands, I looked her dead in the eyes. "I have been gifted two perfect boys," I told her. "And the only people more blessed than me are the two young men who are lucky enough to have you as their mother."

In the sweetest sign that I'd managed to talk her down from the ledge, she kissed me. "I just want everything to be perfect," she whispered.

Though I knew she'd never stop trying, she couldn't control everything. It was likely that Ryan was going to continue pushing boundaries, and Adam's cheek would forever remain dimpled, but everything else was subject to change. I had no desire to plan the fairy-tale. I was too busy living it.

Fiona

I enjoy life's little curveballs, especially when they're thrown at someone else. In a twist I never saw coming, Gill Nicholson had recently got engaged. In a twistier twist than that, she was marrying Trevor flippin' Hillman.

Charlene broke the news to me during one of our gossipy weekly phone calls. "He proposed over a kebab at the Bridge End café," she revealed. "They've been seeing each other since Christmas."

"How is that possible?" I asked in disbelief. "She used to call him the Dickhead of Denton."

"Well, now she's going to be Mrs Dickhead, and we have to be happy for them."

Her salty tone demanded an instant apology from me. "I am happy for them," I assured her. "I'm just surprised."

"Are you sure you're not a tiny bit jealous?" she asked, quietening her voice as pity set in. "I'm sorry you haven't made it down the aisle yet but – "

"Nowt to feel sorry for, Charl." I cut her off with northerner sass that I hadn't used in years. "My life is ace just as it is."

I was telling the absolute truth. The reason why we hadn't tied the knot wasn't a sad tale of discontent. My dream of a princess wedding still held a place in my heart but somewhere along the line, the notion of diamante and pearl wedding dresses had given way to diapers and bottles.

Ryan's arrival brought a shift in priorities, and now that Adam was here, any talk of weddings had been pushed even further onto the backburner.

To those who knew us well, it was a strange turn of events. We are both traditionalists, but there are no awards given for conformity. We were going to take our time and build a strong foundation for our sons, the likes of which neither of us had seen growing up.

The only person who didn't question it was Thierry. He didn't give a damn about the state of our union – or anything else we had going on. I could count the number of times he'd seen Ryan on one hand – and he'd never even met Adam.

Self-absorbed as always, he wasn't the least bit enamoured by his darling grandbabies, but it wasn't a notion that troubled me. I would've been content to permanently fall out of contact, but Jean-Luc is a better son than his father ever deserved. Once a month, he'd make a point of calling him, if only for proof of life.

It always started promisingly. They'd spend a few minutes engaging in polite conversation, and then Thierry would ruin it by saying something offensive and nasty.

Jean-Luc never bit back. He'd simply bow out of the conversation and end the call. Hanging up was all it took to get rid of Thierry, but my mam was much more persistent.

There was no escape when it came to her views on marriage. In her eyes, I was leading a life of debauchery, and it was entirely Jean-Luc's fault.

When I called to let her know that I was coming home to attend Gill's wedding, it took all of three seconds for the conversation to turn ugly.

"When are *you* getting married, my girl?"

She didn't pause long enough for me to answer, which was good because I didn't have one.

"It's the French way, you know," she blasted down the phone. "Perfectly happy to eat the bleedin' steak, but they don't want to pay for it." I had no idea what steak had to do with marriage, but it was her analogy and she was sticking with it. "I want to see the boys but don't bring Jean-Luc with you," she snapped. "Bring me some of those petite four things instead. They're delicious."

"*Petit fours, maman*," I corrected in my best French drawl.

"Whatever," she replied. "But leave the steak thief at home."

When I finally escaped and hung up the phone, I realised Jean-Luc had been hanging on every word, and he wasn't exactly perturbed by the snub.

"I might never marry you now," he said, chuckling like a demon. "Her scorn makes for wonderful entertainment."

I slumped down on the edge of the bed and groaned in exasperation. "She's impossible."

Jean-Luc reached for my hands and pulled me to my feet. "She's slightly tyrannical," he mildly agreed. "But it could be worse."

"How?"

"She could behave like Thierry."

"True," I conceded, linking my arms around his neck. "I just wish she wasn't so heavy handed with her opinions. I would never railroad my sons like that."

A slow smile crept across his perfect face. "You should never say never," he replied. "One day the shoe may be on the other foot. Your son might bring home a girl who makes it her life's work to ruffle your feathers. Then what will you do?"

I thought for a moment, trying to imagine it. More than anything, I wanted my boys to lead happy, sensible lives. Any threat to that would never be tolerated. "I would draw my sword and prepare for battle," I finally conceded.

His grinned broadened. "Which is why you should be more sympathetic to your mother's plight."

"You're not a steak thief, Jean-Luc," I grumbled, fidgeting with a button on his shirt.

He tilted my head, shifting my gaze to his face. "I can handle her, Fiona."

"She calls the boys wild oat babies," I said sourly. "Born on the wrong side of the blanket."

Jean-Luc wasn't appalled by the revelation because he was looking at the bigger picture. Mam had no problem with him per se, and she loved Ryan and Adam to pieces. She was just frustrated, and it brought out the worst in her.

All we had to do to stop the nonsense and placate her was get married, and because neither of us were ready to take the leap, riding out her tantrums was the only option we had.

"A few years from now, this will all be ancient history," he promised. "The wild oat babies will never know what a hard taskmaster their grandmother was in the early days."

His wily grin was infectious. "I hope you're right, Napoleon."

"Of course I'm right," he said, holding me tighter. "Full disclosure is not necessary, Fi. I've already compiled a list of things that the boys will never hear about."

"A list?" My eyes widened in surprise. "What else is on the list?"

"Well, it would do Ryan no good to learn that he was named after the lead character in a book called *Whispered Desires.*" He wiggled his eyebrows like a vaudeville villain.

"We should probably keep that to ourselves, don't you agree?"

"Yes." I couldn't contain my laugh. "But he was a side character and you said you were okay with it."

"I am," he replied. "Ryan is a fine name."

"What else?"

"The dimple farce," he answered in a flash. "Adam needn't find out that you spent an afternoon thinking he was defective. Information like that could ruin a boy."

I pressed myself against his chest, craning my neck to look at him. "Plenty of things could ruin a boy," I uttered suggestively. "He might run into a random girl on the street, fall desperately in love and suddenly find himself smack-bang in the middle of a fairy-tale."

He dipped his head and kissed me in a way that reminded me why I was the luckiest woman in the world.

"One can only hope he's that lucky," he whispered.

London Weekly reported that Princess Di is having a hard time. Supposedly, she's disenchanted, restless and fast becoming known as a royal misfit.

If it's true, I think it's a crying shame.

I guess not every fairy-tale can be perfect, but mine is pretty flippin close.

Today I married the man who makes my toes curl, and if London Weekly decide to write about it, I hope they stick to the truth:

The wedding was grand.

The bride and groom are meant to be.

And they will live happily ever after.

The End

DIARY OF FIONA DÉCARIE

SUNDAY AUGUST 14, 1988

London Weekly reported that Princess Di is having a hard time.
Supposedly, she's disenchanted, restless and fast becoming known
as a royal misfit.
If it's true, I think it's a crying shame.
I guess not every fairy-tale can be perfect, but mine is pretty flippin
close.
Today I married the man who makes my toes curl, and if London
Weekly decide to write about it, I hope they stick to the truth:
The wedding was grand.
The bride and groom are meant to be.
And they will live happily ever after.

The End

CONTACT THE AUTHOR

www.facebook.com/gjwalkersmith
mailto:gjwalkersmith@gmail.com
www.gjwalkersmith.com